Blinding Lights

Jessica Florence

This is a work of fiction. Names, Places, Characters, and Events are fictitious in every regard. Any similarities to actual events, and persons, living or dead, are purely coincidental. Any trademarks, service marks, product names, or named features are assumed to be the property of their respective owners, and are used only for reference. There is no implied endorsement if any of those terms are used. Except for review purposes, the reproduction of this book in whole or part, electronically or mechanically, constitutes a copyright violation.

Jessica Florence © August 2016
Editing by Indie Romance Editing
Lyrics by Author MA Scott

ISBN-13:
978-1530992638

ISBN-10:
153099263X

Prologue

The speakers started playing a piano melody. At the first word of the song, Lily walked onto the stage, one foot in front of the other as her hands gracefully moved beside her. I watched her long starlight colored hair flow as she started to sway. Her head cast down. She rolled her body and stuck her long leg in the air behind her then spun in a circle. The material of her dancer's skirt flowed around her like a pinwheel.

Her head went back down conveying sorrow. I wanted to lift her chin up. She should not be looking down, her beautiful amethyst eyes deserved to be seen. I hadn't seen her dance since we were teens. I felt enraptured by her.

My eyes were glued as the singer started bellowing out the chorus. Her head whipped back again as she leapt into the air and spun. She landed on one foot, and her hands moved around her like a swan. I felt every bit of the emotions in my soul from the song through her dance. It was as if she herself was giving life to the words with every move of her body. She leapt, spun, and bounced around. She swayed back and forth as if she was being pulled between two forces.

    My heart ached for her. The emotions in this dance were ones of devastation and regret. She fell to the ground lying on her back then her chest came up then fell back slowly, as if trying to bring herself back to life. Her hair swirled around her in soft waves. She got back up quickly and twirled to the back on the stage. With the last bit of the song, she ran and jumped into the air, spread her legs into a split into the air and landed. She gave it her all, she threw everything she had into the emotions of this dance. At the end she fell to the ground and crumpled.

    I wanted to run to her, scoop her up, and tell her everything. But she could never be mine. I'd given up that dream years ago. I wasn't even sure why I had stopped by to see her perform. I almost wish I hadn't. To see her move with that much passion, so much that I could only dream to possess an ounce of it. I spared one last look at her as I stood. The crowd had erupted into cheers and screams in applause for her performance. She was smiling while flowers were placed in her hands as she took a bow to her audience.

Tears glistened on her rosy cheeks. She had such a powerful spirit in everything she did.

Not able to take anymore I turned and left the cheers and the woman I loved behind me. My soul was stained black with death. Someone as bright and pure as my Lily, deserved more. I think I had convinced myself if I saw her again that maybe I would change my mind to pursue her. To finally find peace in my life, but only to see her and feel just as I did when I left a few years ago. Devastated.

I walked out of the auditorium building promising myself that I wouldn't try to see her anymore. It was just torture on my soul. I had to give her up completely. The hope of having Lily was left back on that stage with her.

I had jobs to do, that would be my only salvation in this hell of a life.

I got on my bike and sped off as far away from my starlight as I could.

Chapter One
Six years later
Lachlan

I watched the two men guarding the door to the building I needed to get into from the cover of the truck I was under. I had been lying there, waiting for the right moment. It would be any second now. Both men were loosely holding their guns while smoking cigarettes. I wanted to shoot both of them and be done but that wasn't my job this time. No, this was an extraction job. Get in and rescue three girls that were taken from their villa in Spain. One of the girl's father was a powerful man in politics, which was no surprise how he found my number.

I was a mercenary for hire. However, I didn't take just any jobs. I was the elite. I was the one you called when you needed no prints to lead back to you. Do the dirty work and do it well.

This shit hole in front of me was a flesh factory. Men would kidnap women and keep them there. Men would take their turns using them and then they would sell them off in the black market. I wanted to blow this place to bits, but that wasn't why I was here. I had a job to do.

The two dumbasses gave me my opportunity to move in when they went to the bushes to piss, like two women going to the bathroom together. They really didn't think anyone would attempt to do something here. Shaking my head at their stupidity, I cradled my gun in my hands and crawled out from under the truck. With the skills of a trained assassin, I moved with stealth and opened the door to the building. There were one or two empty rooms before I hit a massive room filled with sheet-walled cubicles. Sick.

The sounds of moans and subtle no's fill the room. I gritted my teeth so hard I thought I would break them.

Not my job.

I walked down the hall, slowly peeking and looking for the girls. I shut down my mind and focused solely on my objective. I couldn't tear this place apart and get the girls out safely. Sometimes I hated parts of my job.

A man stepped out from one of the cubicles tucking his junk back in his pants. Fucker. His eyes widened at seeing me, but before he could mouth off my hands shot out and twisted his neck. One scumbag down, two million more to go. I gripped his body and pulled him into an empty cubicle area. I checked back into the little makeshift hallway and walked back out in search of the girls.

I found them huddled together on a bed. I took in their appearance to make sure they were the women from the photos I was given. Yep, they were.

I opened the sheet curtain and their pale faces were stricken with fear. Fuck.

"My name is Lachlan, I'm here to rescue you girls. Are any of you hurt?" I didn't see any visible signs of injury. They shook their head, but still looked like they couldn't trust me. Can't blame them there.

"Look, I was hired by Angela's father to get you out. We need to get a move on and you have to listen to everything I say." I willed them to understand and trust me. The girl in the middle with blonde hair spoke up with a shaky voice.

"We understand." Slowly the girls got up while I peeked outside their curtain. A few other men were leaving and two more had come in. I listened while they talked about one girl they both wanted to have a go at, but couldn't because she was spoken for. Every once in a while that would happen where one of the girls they took was taken for a specific purpose. Usually a virgin to be sold to the highest bidder. I looked at the girls behind me to make sure they were ready to go. All three of their heads bobbed up and down.

    Go time.

    I parted the curtain and together we moved through the hall of horror. A man opened the door and I gestured for the girls to move into a cubicle I had deemed empty moments before. I joined them and watched as the man walked to the back of the giant room and entered through another door. I turned back to look at the girls when something behind them caught my eye.

    If there was ever a moment in my life where I felt like I was going to die, that moment was it. My heart dried and crumbled. My rage soared. I walked over to the side of the small bed and pushed the bright starlight hair out of her face. Lily.

    The same Lily, whose face, has plagued my heart since I was a wee lad. What the fuck was she doing here? I looked over and saw an IV sticking out of her arm. I checked the bag. They were doping her up. Fucking hell.

Decision was made, as soon as my job was done I was killing every last one of these fuckers. I looked back at the face of my Angel. No, that was wrong. She was never mine. Her face held no sunshine in it, she was wearing the same clothes they probably took her in which gave me some inclination that she hadn't been here long. I prayed she hadn't been used like some of the others in this place.

As gently as I could, I pulled the IV out of her arm and watched as she did not even flinch. She was out cold. I scooped her up and threw her on my shoulder, no way in hell was I leaving her here. I looked at the girls and spoke.

"Let's get the fuck out of here." I hoisted my gun and was ready to go.

I got the girls out pretty easily. Only having to kill the two men guarding the door, but that was mostly because I was pissed they had Lily and I wanted blood. I had a truck waiting for us about a mile away. Once everyone was safely inside, Lily lying across the bench seat into my lap, I sped off towards the plane that would take us back to the states.

There was a medic on the plane, ready to assist the girls in any way they needed. As soon as I told the girls to get checked out, they insisted they were fine and to have him check out Lily. I wasn't going to press the issue. I wanted to make sure she was ok.

I phoned the father and let him know his packages were safe and on their route home. As soon as we land, they would be put into a black SUV then taken home. As for Lily, hell I didn't know what I was going to do. I didn't really want anyone else to watch over her, but damn if I was going to put myself in her proximity for any extended amount of time. It was hard enough being near her now. I wanted to hold her, kiss her, let her in. But I couldn't. There was no use torturing myself, but what a sweet torture it would be. Shaking my head, I went to work on erasing myself from the cyber networks that help me find the girls. No traces.

When we were close to landing I checked on the girls, all were fine, and staying quiet. What they had been through was a huge deal. I'm sure they would have their moments to really take in what they had survived later. The doctor came and sat next to me a few minutes later.

"So?" He didn't need to know what I was asking about. He knew.

"She's been heavily sedated with heroin. They wanted her completely unaware of her surroundings. After my exam, it seems they hadn't abused her physically or sexually which is a blessing since she is such a petite girl." I looked back to the small girl lying on the bed. She was always petite. She had the body of a dancer, her legs were toned, her waist small, and her breasts were barely a palm full. She was perfect.

"Is she going to be ok?" I didn't realize I was holding my breath until he answered.

"It's not going to be pretty to get the heroin out of her system. I would suspect mentally after some counseling, she will be back to normal." He looked confident and I was satisfied.

"I looked up the name you had given me. She used to have family in Florida, and has an emergency contact New York. I suggest you let them know you have found her. Lay to rest some weary minds." He gave me a nod and went back to Lily, checking the IV he had placed in her arm. Who the hell was the emergency contact in New York? A roommate? A boyfriend? Or worse, a husband?

I hadn't let myself give into the urge to check up on her. She deserved a happy life. I hated the feeling of my gut twisting thinking about her with another man. My thoughts were interrupted by the plane's dissension. I had to finish this job, then I would figure out what I was going to do with Lily.

I grabbed my jacket as we landed. New York in the winter was pretty brutal. I needed to take care of the girls when the doors open. As expected, a black suburban was parked where we came to a stop. The bodyguard for the girls stepped out and checked them over as we walked down the stairs. They all hugged him and got in the car. The daughter had turned and spoke.

"Thank you, Lachlan." I nodded as my reply. There were no words necessary. I walked over to the bodyguard, he handed me an envelope with the cash for my services. He gave me a nod and turned to leave. I watched as they drove off and looked back at the plane.

I hadn't had much thought to what I was going to do with Lily, though I feel like I should take her to a hospital and call her mom to let them know she was ok. Not having any jobs that needed my immediate action, I walked back up into the plane. The doctor was taking the IV out, shaking his head.

"Poor girl. I suggest you take her to the hospital so they can help get the drugs out of her system." That finalized my decision. I would take her and then I would get out of there, hopefully before she woke up.

I scooped her up and carried her down to an SUV that was left for me. I watched as the doctor got into his own sedan and drove off. Lightly setting Lily in the back and buckling her, I hopped in the driver's seat and sped off.

Chapter Two
Lachlan

The doctors at the hospital flew into action and pushed lots of fluids into her system. I grabbed a cup of coffee and waited just to make sure everything was ok. The hospital staff had called the emergency contact. I convinced myself not to locate the owner of that number to see if she was involved. I wasn't privy to that information anymore.

Feeling the adrenaline start to die from tonight's events, I closed my eyes and let myself rest. I thought about the first time I saw Lily when we were kids. She was beautiful even then. Her long blonde hair reminded me of the stars. She was little and almost frail looking, but she had spirit and was no one to push around. She would get in fights with girls in school who would make fun of her amethyst eyes. The doctors said it was an abnormality but I always thought it made her unique and special. We used to play with Wolfe all the time too. The three of us. I knew a smile graced my lips when I thought about how I caught that asshat Lee Briggs bragging about making out with her in her freshman year. Wolfe and I made sure he apologized to her and after that she didn't have much luck finding dates. That was a sorry, not sorry moment. Only my Ma and Wolfe knew I was in love with her. Wolfe called it immediately, same with Ma. My four other brothers teased me for being such friends with her but never realizing it. They never figured it out.

"Lachlan." A soft voice moaned, my eyes flew open and looked at the girl lying on the bed.

Her eyes were shut, her eyebrows pinched together. Had she called out my name in her sleep? I was up and moving towards her instantly. My hand shot out and I lightly ran my fingers along her cheek. God, she was so beautiful. She moved her head into my hand. Her eyebrows relaxed. I felt the tingles in my chest but put a stop to it. I removed my hand just as her eyes fluttered open. She looked around, her frightened expression sobered me up even more.

When her eyes settled on me, I was unprepared for the feelings that assaulted me. I wanted to kiss her, tell her of my love, and never let her go. Recognition flared in those jeweled depths.

"Lach?" She croaked out. Her sweet voice was so hoarse right now. I flinched.

"Yeah Lily bug." I used her nickname from our childhood, setting us back in the friend zone before we even started talking.

"What happened?" She asked, I really did not want to be the one to tell her about everything, only because it made my blood boil to think about the way she looked on that bed in that shit hole.

"What do you remember?" She closed her eyes, thinking.

"I was on my way to my performance in Milan. I.. I remember someone grabbing me, and now I'm here." Her words both eased me and enraged me. I was pissed she was taken like that, but so glad she didn't remember anything that occurred after. If there was a God, I prayed that she never got any delayed memories from her stay there.

"Why are you here?" She whispered.

"I rescued you. What? Not happy to see me Lily bug?" I flashed her a smile. She rolled her eyes. She was about to say something when a male voice cried out from the door.

"Lily!" A man rushed over to her and touched her face much like how I had. I made my body relax even though I wanted to remove his hand, as taking a step back to my seat. He leaned down to press his lips to hers, I turned my head, not wanting to see that. When my head turned back towards them, I was met with her questioning gaze.

"You must be Lachlan. I can't thank you enough for rescuing my Lily." His hand shot forward for a shake. His Lily? I was about to tell him she was my Lily, but swallowed it down.

"Yeah, that's me." I shook his hand, maybe putting in a little extra force behind the grip. He pulled his hand back and shook it at his side before turning back to Lily. I looked him over while they talked. He was a few inches shorter than my 6'3. Unlike my cut brown hair, his was shaggy and blonde. His eyes were blue and mine were green. He was the exact opposite of me. He was wearing a suit and tie, an office type of guy. You couldn't keep me in an office even if I was forced by gun point. I knew she has probably had a bunch of boyfriends over the years. As much as the thought hurt, I did want her to live a happy life. This dick better make her happy.

"Lachlan." Lily's voice broke through my thoughts.

"What's up?" I looked at her, while her boyfriend gave her a kiss and walked out of the room. Weird.

"You rescued me? How?" She was sitting up, waiting eagerly to hear my answers. Hmm, this would be interesting. She didn't know what I did, it wasn't something I broadcasted to the world.

"You were taken by bad people, I rescued you. You're safe now. That's all you gotta know." I told her. She pursed her lips but remained silent. I know she wanted to ask more, but knew she couldn't push me. We sat there for a few minutes in silence, just staring into each other's eyes.

"Why?" Her voice was so soft, barely above a whisper. Her question was loaded. Why did I leave when she kissed me? Why I hadn't I tried to contact her since then? Why? Why? I didn't know what to say. Probably the only moment I would have been thankful for her having a boyfriend was right now. He walked in the door, so I didn't have to answer her question. Her eyes were pleading with me, as much as I wanted to tell her, I wouldn't. It was time for me to leave. She was safe, and being taken care of. I couldn't infect her with my darkness any more. She would move on, maybe marry this guy, have babies. All things I could never do.

"Alright, well Lily bug. You are well taken care of now. I'm gonna head out." I gave her my best heart breaker smile. Hiding the pain of leaving her behind again.

"You're leaving me again?" She was hurting, it was all I ever did around her.

"Bye bug." I looked her over one last time then walked out the door. I got in the SUV and drove to a hotel. I grabbed my bag, got a key, and rented the cheap room. I jumped into the shower and washed the grime off of me. I didn't let myself think of Lily. It only made my heart hurt, well what little a heart I had left. While the water ran over my back, I thought about what my next move was going to be. Take another job? Vacation? Get pissed at the bar? Go home? I thought about home, it had been about a year since I dropped in to see my family. We were still a close family, minus my oldest brother Roderick, he died when I was eighteen. Moving away from those thoughts, I decided going home would be a good thing. Christmas was in a few days, maybe Wolfe and Nera would be there. It had been a few months since I had seen my friend and my little warrior. She always rolled her eyes and demanded I told her what Laoch meant when I said it, she thought I was teasing her. It meant warrior. She was a warrior, after everything she went through she deserved the name. Why she hadn't just looked it up on google was beyond me. Maybe she liked our game.

    I finished my shower and dried off, I turned off all of my devices, threw the towel on the floor and fell onto the bed. I was beat, and passed out quickly.

    I dreamed of her dancing. Her starlight hair flowing around her while she twirled. In my dream, she noticed me mid-spin. That bright smile lit up her face. She ran to me and launched her body into my arms. She pressed her lips to mine and I kissed her back. She was mine. We smiled and held onto each other like nothing else in the world mattered.

    When I woke up, I stared at the ceiling of the cheap hotel. I left Lily behind, again. It was the right thing; she has no clue what kind of man I was. If she did, she would run far away from me. I was dangerous. I could kill a man with a toothpick, if I wanted. You name it, I've done it. Things her pure heart should never be around. I rolled over and turned on my phone. I had a job request but it wasn't until two weeks from now. Hmm, head home for two weeks, then go on the job. That would work. I looked over the details, it looked simple enough. I would mull it over again later. I had to set up a flight and head back to Scotland. But first, I was heading back to that shit hole. Some fuckers needed to die, like yesterday.

Chapter Three
Lachlan

    The smell of fresh bacon and eggs woke me from my slumber. I rolled onto my back and looked up at the ceiling. The same ceiling I stared at in my youth wondering what my life was going to be like after high school. I think I was planning on being an officer of the law. That obviously didn't pan out the way I had wanted.

    I killed all of those men that had a part in taking Lily. They deserved it. The other girls who hadn't died were released and looked over by the firetrucks and paramedics that had been called. It eased part of my soul to know I had done some good by killing so many. There was no remorse in me, that wasn't something you would find. I enjoyed watching the light leave those men's eyes. I heard chatter downstairs and immediately my mood improved. I had snuck into my family's home last night.

One thing that has never changed in me was the joy of surprising my mother. I lived to make her shriek, then break out into those happy tears. I still like to scare her every once in a while, jump out behind corners, things like that. She was too easy. Although you would think with six kids, she would have had skin thick as a rhino. Nope, my mama was a big old softy.

I got up out of bed, and stretched. My muscles were aching like hell. I grabbed a t-shirt from my drawer, tightened the strings on my sweat pants, and quietly snuck down the stairs. A big shit eating grin on my face. I listened around the corner of the hallway to see who was all in the room with her.

"Ma, Ah want tae go tae Brandon's today. That ok with ye?" My youngest brother Aiden spoke. I missed their Scottish brogue. He was twelve the youngest. He was an oops baby, hell I was 14 when he was born. But he was a cool kid. I had fun playing with him when I came home.

"Of course, just make sure ye are back for dinner." Mom replied. I heard the scraping of a few plates, some of the other's must be there. Taking a short peek into the kitchen I saw mama cooking on the stove, Aiden was sitting at the table eating a big piece of bacon. No sign of

Findley, Grant, or Pa. Truthfully, I shouldn't have expected them here. They all had lives. Pa was probably at work, fixing cars. Findley was most likely with him. Grant was probably with his family, a wife and two twin girls. He was the oldest since Roderick died when I was 18.

    Well now was as great a time as any to shock Ma. Casually I walked into the kitchen and spoke calmly.

    "Smells good, Ma. Load me up with a plate will ya?" I walked up behind her and she shrieked while jumping in a circle to see me.

    "Lachlan ye shit head! What the hell are ye doing home?" She launched herself into my arms for a tight hug.

    "I needed a break, thought I'd surprise ya." Pulling back, I kissed Ma on her brownish grey haired head.

    "I see a few more grey's there, Ma. Aiden giving you a hard time." I turned to my brother and winked at him. He just shook his head but walked over for a hug. I ruffled his hair as he let go of the hug.

    "Kicking ass and taking names?" I asked him, kind of my way of saying how's it going. I knew it was coming but I flinched anyways. The pop to the back of my head from Ma was expected. I had missed this playfulness. It was a break from the killings, and pain. Ma went back to cooking and talking a mile a minute. I made myself a plate of food and listened as she told me about everything I had missed in the past year. Grant's girls were on the soccer team for their school. I tried to imagine five year olds playing soccer but all I thought of was them chasing butterflies or running the wrong way. Pa and Findley were working on two classic cars right now. Restoration job, guy wanted them fixed up for a big show. Aiden was doing good in school, all A's. "Such a sweet boy" She cooed. Aiden looked like he wanted to be swallowed up by the earth at her comment.

"Oh, and we are going tae throw a party for Roderick's 30th birthday, Ah hope ye will still be here for that." She gave me the lip, and the puppy eyes. As much as I didn't want to be here for that, I nodded yes. She got all giddy and started cleaning the kitchen. Ma was a stay at home mom, she worked hard keeping us boys in line, and taking care of the couple farm animals we had. I could tell time was starting to wear on her though. She looked like she was losing a little weight, her hair was more grey than brown, her green eyes were like mine, but were looking a little dull. It was unlike her. I looked at Aiden to see him playing on his phone, unaware if something was bothering Ma. It looked like I would have to figure some shit out while I was here.

The rest of the day I helped Ma with whatever she needed, then went for a walk around the property. My family lived in the outskirts of Portree on a very peaceful nine acres. It was a little brisk but I didn't mind the chill. I welcomed it to distract me from thinking about what was going on with Ma, or more to distract me from thinking about Lily. I had thought about how she was doing, were the drugs out of her system already? Then my thoughts drifted towards her boyfriend, which made me want to break his hands for touching her. So it was best if I didn't think of her.

Later when Pa and Findley came home, they were both surprised to see me, but quickly jumped into conversations about the new corvette they were working on. It sounded cool. Mechanics was never something I was into, Pa tried but it just wasn't me. Ma had called Grant so he came over for dinner with his family. His wife Jenny, and the girls, Jenson and Jossilyn, seemed a little scared of me and ran to their dad when I waved hi. I figured they would come around eventually. Could kids see the darkness inside someone? If so, I was fucked at getting to know my nieces.

It was nice to have everyone in the same room together. All my brothers except me and Roderick had taken after Pa, with reddish hair with brown eyes. We were all tall though, towering over Ma's five foot three.

By the time everyone had settled down and Grant's family left to get the girls into bed, I was beat tired. I took a quick shower and collapsed on my old creaky bed. Not really having a choice, my mind drifted to sleep with thoughts of my starlight girl. The bright light that could never be mine.

Chapter Four
Lily

"I'm really sorry. You've been amazing, and I care for you a lot. I just can't give you my heart, it's never been mine to give." I hated to admit it to Lance. He was an amazing boyfriend. We had been together for six months and he was great. He was patient, and didn't care that I travelled a lot for work. I just couldn't do it anymore. Not after seeing Lachlan, I wasn't going to let it go any longer.

"I get it." Lance's voice was sad but he looked at me, giving me an it's ok smile. God I wished I could love him. My life would be so easy, well as long as his creepy brother, and crazy sister stayed away. His brother was a doctor and tried to see me in the hospital but I was like, meh no. He just wanted to touch me a little too much. And his sister was just a nut. But, that didn't matter anymore. I would be grabbing a few of the things that I brought over to Lance's apartment and going home.

"I really am sorry." I didn't know what else to say. I gave him a kiss on the forehead and grabbed my things.

"I know we are broken up now, but if you ever need anything, or change your mind." I smiled weakly at his words. Such a sweet man.

"You'll be the first person I call." It wasn't false hope. I just couldn't tell him that it would never happen. I'd been in love with Lachlan since I first saw him when we were younger. He'd always treated me like a little sister, and while that hurt, I never let it stop me. That was until I tried for more and then he avoided me for eight years till the night he saved me. Even then he ran like I was one of the walking dead. But I was done letting him avoid me. If he truly didn't want me then fine, he was going to say it to my face. But something inside me kept telling me that wasn't the case. He loved me too, he was just too into his own self to see it.

On the cab ride back to my apartment I thought about seeing him in the hospital. He was so different. The day before he left my world he was care free, a rebel, but always smiled. He would tease me all the time but would kick anyone's ass if they tried to tease me. He and Wolfe were always so protective of me. It ruined any chance I had for dating in high school, which turned out to be good anyways. I always wanted him and it gave me more time to focus on my dancing. Seeing him in that hospital was like anything I could have expected.

He looked dangerous. He had an edge to him that said he could mess you up for looking at him the wrong way. His face was harder, but it didn't ease the flame inside me that burned for him. Oh no. In fact, I felt ten times hotter. Everything about him screamed, I'm bad news. But to me that was a siren's call. I wanted him more than ever. Hence my reasons for what I was about to do.

The cab stopped at my building, I paid the man and carried my stuff into the warm lobby and up to my apartment. I had a few calls to make, then booked my flight to Scotland. Clicking that button to confirm I had wanted to pay for that flight felt like I was making the biggest choice in my life. Bigger than when I had signed on with one of the largest dance companies in the world. This was a step towards the future I had dreamed of. My future with the man I loved. I would do whatever it took.

Feeling pretty great about everything, I decided to go take a bubble bath and soak. My body was still feeling a little off from everything that had happened but I was better than yesterday, and the day before that. I knew I'd be ok. I started the water on my bath and shed my clothes. I lit a couple of the candles around my tub and pour into the bubble mixture. For an added kick, I scooped out a cup of Epsom salt to help detox my body. A moan escaped my lips once my body was submerged in the water. It felt heavenly. I slowly wiggled, letting my body soak in the warmth.

    My thoughts once again drifted to the dangerous man from the other day. He gave me nothing in his green eyes. No true warmth, no looks of disgust. Nothing. I wanted to see desire, and love in them. There were a few times back in our younger days, I thought I had seen it. And when he said he had saved me. How had he saved me?

    The doctors told me that I had been taken by people and drugged, most likely to be sold on the flesh market. I was shocked to find that out. I mean, I knew it happened, but you don't really think it would happen to you. Thankfully after a full exam, the results showed I had not been raped or abused. Tears sprang free from me after that announcement. It was nothing I could have ever expected, but how in the world could Lachlan have saved me. I mean those were bad, bad people, with guns, and probably tanks for all I knew. I was so confused. I needed answers. I needed answers to everything when it came to him.

I felt that smile of mischief lift my lips. I may be a dancer, and look sweet as sugar, but I was a hellion all on my own. Lachlan had no clue what was about to happen. All I thought about was he was going to get the holiday of a lifetime. I wiggled until I was under the water all the way. It was like all of those books I read. But instead of the man chasing the woman, I would be chasing him. This plan of mine was sounding better and better the more I thought of it.

Once the water started to turn a little cold, I got out and dressed, then I settled onto the couch. I had one more call to make. I found the number on my phone and pressed call. It ringed twice before he answered.

"Wolfe." I smiled at his answer.

"Aw, I've missed you too you. How's my favorite rock star? Still whisking your lady around the world on your tours?" I heard him chuckle on the other line. Wolfe and I continued to stay friends over the years. I was hurting hard when everything happened with Alexis and the baby. I flew out to see him when it happened. He was devastated. I was a little worried when he had told me about Nera, she was fighting his affections for a while. I was worried he would get hurt again, but it turned out to be the best thing that ever happened to him. He had his soulmate.

"She's loving every minute of it." He told me. I could see her rolling her eyes at his comment. She was a cool girl.

"I bet. So I have some really awesome news, are you ready for this? I'm not sure you are." I was practically bouncing on the couch.

"Ah guess." I ignored his lack of enthusiasm and told him anyways.

"I'm leaving for Portree Christmas eve!" I screamed. I heard more chuckling on the other line.

"Ah see, visiting the motherland for any particular reason. Besides visiting Nera and Ah?" Wolfe knew about my love for Lachlan, and he never gave me any inside intel when it came to the man. But I tried to use him as a double agent on a few occasions.

" Have you talked to Lachlan lately?" I asked, curious.

"He texted me a bit ago. Said he was in town. Why?"

"I didn't know if you had heard. Now before I tell you, you have to promise not to freak?" I guess I should have thought this phone call through more. Wolfe would freak about me getting taken. Nera was taken by her step-parents back when they first started out together and he went berserk. Obviously that worked out ok. I never knew how she got out, just that she did.

"No, but yer gonna tell me anyways." Figures. Well there was no turning back now.

"I was taken, while on my way to Milan. I don't remember any of it. They had drugged me and I woke up in the hospital. Lachlan was there, he said he had saved me. Then he left. I feel a lot better, and everything is ok. I'm ok. But I need to see him. I need answers." I took a pause.

"I'm also done waiting for him. I'm going to fight for him, Wolfe." It was nice to voice my plan out loud. I waited for him to say something. But the line was quiet. Had I hung up on him accidentally? I looked at my phone, nope still connected.

"Wolfe?"

"Ye were taken?" His voice was hard. I bit my lip.

"Yeah, but everything is ok. Did you hear that part? What about the part about me going after Lachlan?" I was trying to move away from the taken part.

"Aye. Ah will be getting ye a stun gun as soon as ye gets into town. Maybe some self-defense classes with Nera. Fucking woman in mah life being taken. Not gonna happen anymore."

I shook my head. Always so protective, but I wasn't going to tell him no. Truthfully, that all sounded good. I figured getting taken was like getting hit by lightning, it probably wouldn't happen again. But I'd rather have some defense if it does.

"Ok." I agreed. No fight there.

"Ah will see ye in Portree, text me when ye're in."

"What about the Lachlan thing? Any words for me?" I was hoping he would say It's about time, or something.

"Aye, don't give up. Love is always worth the fight. No matter how stubborn the mind may be, the heart always wins." With that, he said he had to go and we disconnected. I burned those words into my mind. I would be doing just that. Not giving up. Lachlan was mine, he always was.

Chapter Five
Lachlan

"Aw come on wee bro. Give up, we all know ye ain't got it in ya." Grant commented. Us brothers were playing poker around the table. Findley, and Aiden had folded. It was between me and Grant. Winner took home twenty bucks, three sugar cookies, and choice of dinner for tonight. Grant thought he had the win in the bag. Well, I learned to be good at poker in my travels over the years. He didn't stand a chance.

"Do it Lach, kick his ass." Aiden piped up. I heard the smack of his head from ma. I wanted to laugh but I kept my face stoic. Grant laid down his cards.

"Full house, wee bro. Ah think we will be having Haggis tonight." He teased. It was a good hand, but alas I would win. I always won. Without taking my eyes off of his, I lowered my cards. I heard a few hoots and gasps but kept my eyes on Grant. I relished in the moment as his eyes looked down at my cards. His head fell back and he stood up.

"Seriously, ye had tae be cheating!" He started pacing. It was hard not to laugh, so I did. I had been back in Scotland for a few days and tonight was Christmas eve. We weren't really doing anything as a family, just hanging out. The girls were talking about what they were going to get from Santa. It was nice to be surrounded by happy people. Almost naive to what all was happening in the world, thing I dealt with daily.

The sound of a knock on the door echoed around the room. I looked at Ma as she got up to go answer it. I wondered who would be coming in. I slowly reached around my back and gripped the handle of my gun that I had stashed behind my waistband. Ready for danger. I heard Ma scream only to be followed by what sounded like tears. I jumped up, about to run to her when she entered the kitchen with someone behind her. Her face was lit up with happy tears.

"Look who just showed up." She moved to the side revealing the guest.

"Lily." Her name slipped from my lips on a whisper. I was stunned, why was she here? She looked around and waved at everyone. The family snapped out of their shock and swarmed her. Giving her hug after hug. I didn't know what to do. Playing the game that I hadn't seen her in a while, I put on my poker face from earlier.

"Lily bug." I saw her flinch, but I walked up and engulfed her in a hug. One of her small arms wrapped around me high, her fingers delving into the hair at the nape of my neck. Her other around my lower back. I sucked in a breath as her breasts were pressed against my chest. She was molded to me. Torture, pure torture. She gave me a kiss on the skin of my neck. My eyes fluttered closed, she was killing me. Shivers ran down my body and back up right to my cock. I felt it start to stir to life. Time to pull back. I untangled from her arms and took a few steps back, trying to think of anything besides her body against mine. Having a hard on around all of my family was not something I wanted.

"What are ye doing here sweetheart?" Ma spoke up. Lily's hair was pulled up into a bun, she was wearing a sweat shirt that hung down off one shoulder and some legging tucked into boots. For having traveled from New York to Scotland, she looked like a dream. Her cheeks turned pink and I wished I knew what she was blushing about.

"I needed a break from New York, so I thought I would come see my second family. I've missed it here." She smiled at all of us. Her eyes landed on me, she held my gaze for a few moments longer than others. Ma interrupted our stuck gaze by hugging her again.

"How long are ye going tae be in the area? Where are ye staying?" Ma launched into conversation. The rest of the family went on doing other things. I was paying attention to their conversation.

"Um, not sure on how long, and I was going to look for a place to stay after I stopped by here." She tucked a stray piece of her hair behind her ear, it was something she did when she lied. Her cue. I learned that back in high school, she could never fool me.

"Nonsense sweetheart, Ye will stay here in Grant's old room! Let's take yer things up there and let ye get settled. Lachlan, do ye mind if Ah make something special for dinner tonight?" I nodded no. She was staying here? In Grant's old room. Which was right next to mine. It was official, life was still punishing me for the killings and wrong doings of my life. It was the only explanation for her being here and staying so close to me. I went to the fridge and grabbed a beer. This little vacation just turned into hell. I waited until Ma left Lily alone before heading up to her room. I knew she wasn't really here for the reasons she stated, so I wanted the real ones.

She was bent over unzipping her bag when I knocked on the door. She had a fantastic ass, toned, and was the perfect topping to her long, lean dancer legs.

"Come in." She spoke without looking who was at the door. I took a step inside, wishing I could walk up to her and pull her ass back towards me. Instead, I walked and sat on the computer chair to the right of the bed. Grant's room hadn't changed, still boring. Nothing on the walls, except blue wall paper, his desk, and picture of his wife on the desk. He was a minimalist. I looked back at my angel.

"What's the real reason Lily?"

She slowly let go of the clothes she had in her hand and stood up.

"Lachlan." She turned and looked me in the eye. I was very good at reading people. But I was confused by the look on her face. She was determined.

"Why are you really here?" I had to know. She bit her lip and took a step toward me.

"You, I need to talk to you." She kept on walking, suddenly I wished I hadn't trapped myself in this chair. I had nowhere to go. Instead of watching her hips sway towards me, I counted my chances of standing up without it being weird. The numbers weren't good. She stopped in front of me and lowered down to her knees. Holy hell.

I held my breath so I wouldn't groan like I wanted to. Her on her knees in front of me was a dream.

"I want to know the truth about what happened. You said you saved me. How could you have done that?" She looked at me with those beautiful purple eyes. She was pleading with me to be honest with her. It wasn't going to happen. She would, and should run far from me. Especially if she knew the truth.

"Sorry Lily bug, not gonna crack." I told her

"Stop calling me Lily bug, . I'm not a child, I'm a grown woman for Christ's sake." She was annoyed, I liked to rile her up even though she did have a point. She was a beautiful, warm-blooded woman. One that could bring me to my knees, always could.

"Always be Lily bug to me." I wasn't sure what her reaction would be to me teasing but I definitely wasn't expecting her to put her hands on my knees. My jaw hardened, all lightness has left the room.

"What are you doing?" It was hard to keep my voice from showing the pure pleasure I felt from her hands on me, but I managed.

"I missed you so much." She spoke softly as her hands slowly started moving up my thighs, then back down. FUCK!

"I could never get you out of my head, Lachlan. You've always been there with me." Her nails scratched against my jeans as she pulled her hands back down towards my knees. She wanted me, fuck, Lily wanted me. It was clear as day. But I couldn't give in. My cock was growing and begging for her hands to go up a little further. I remained still as stone. Her hands watched me for some sort of reaction. I gave her none.

"Where's your boyfriend, Lily?" I wanted to remind her of him, I was grasping at straws. I didn't want to be a complete dick to her but I had to get her to stop.

"I left him as soon as I got home, there's only one man I want. One man I've ever wanted." I had to get the hell out of there.

"Good for him. You'll always be a lucky catch." My hands gripped hers, stopping her exploration and torture of me.

"You know who I'm talking about Lachlan. You can't keep denying it. I see it in your eyes." She looked at me, daring me to admit it.

"Not gonna happen, Lily." I lightly took her hands off me and stood. Her face was right by my dick. Poor decision to move.

"I'm not letting you go Lachlan, not this time." She stood and leaned up to give me a kiss on the cheek then walked out of the room. Leaving me there with so much shit going on in my head. Lily wanted me. Had wanted me for a long time. What the hell was I going to do? I knew I should leave Scotland. Get the hell out before my resolve cracked, but damn if I didn't want to stay and burn in hell for a drop of her presence.

I felt my cock straining against my zipper, that needed to be taken care of first. Then I would stay, but couldn't let Lily comprise me. She didn't belong in my world. She didn't belong with me. She was too pure, all starlight. I had about one week left before my next job, and then I'd be gone again. I would be a fleeting thought in her head.

Chapter Six
Lachlan

    With hard strides, I walked out of Grant's room and went into mine. I needed a shower and a good stroke to alleviate the pressure from Lily's touch. Grabbing a towel and some clothes to change into, I walked across the hall to the shower we all had to share and stripped down.

    It took maybe five long strokes in the shower before I came on the tiled wall. Lily worked me up and lit me on fire just being near me. I tried to have sex with women after I got into the mercenary business, but meaningless sex was pointless sex. Sure I got off, sometimes, but it wasn't satisfactory. My body knew who it belonged to, it didn't want anyone else. So for years, I haven't cared to find a woman to ease any edge. I took care of myself, it was the only way I could be near her. In my head.

After I was done, I dried off and changed into sweat pants and a t-shirt. I prayed my dick could stay under control while we were around my family.

I put my dirty clothes in the hamper and headed downstairs. Everyone was chatting while Ma cooked dinner. I didn't know what it was but it smelled delicious.

"Lachlan. Glad ye could join us son. Ah was just talking with Lily about that one time ye and Wolfe talked her into eating that pie ye made out of mud and whipped cream." Dad started cracking up with laughter. It was a precious memory I carried of her in my head. We did lots of things to her. Pranks of all sorts. But she always got us back. She was always plotting her revenge.

"That is a good one." I smiled. Laughing about the good old times.

"Remember when I put make up on Lachlan's face before he had a date with Cindy Homer in 9th grade. He should have known better than to take a nap before a date while I was around." Lily retorted with a memory of her own. She wasn't one to take things and not dish it back out. It was one of the many qualities I admired about her. She wasn't afraid, she was brave, and strong. I heard a little nagging in the back of my head saying she was strong enough to be with me. But I quashed it down.

"So Ma, what's for dinner?" I left Lily with dad and went to give Ma a kiss on the cheek. Subtly observing what she was making.

"A surprise. Now move yer tush." She bumped me away. So much for motherly love. I scoffed of fake heartbreak while moving over to another sibling. They were all too busy for their brother. Suckers. I decided it was a time to take a break from people and go outside.

I lived my life for the most part alone. Occasional trips home or stopping by to see my little Laoch and Wolfe were about it. I enjoyed being alone. No one was around to witness the darkness that tended to overcome me. As I sat down at the little table set facing the trees, I cleared my mind, letting go of pain, letting go of happiness, letting it all empty from me.

"You're looking very somber over there. You doing ok?" Lily's voice broke though the silence. I kept my eyes closed and answered her.

"Just clearing my mind."

"I could be there for you, you know. A support system. If only you'd let me in." Her words hit me in the chest. I'd given up hope of a life with her a long time ago. It just wasn't meant to be, despite me longing for that life with all of my being.

"I don't know what you're talking about Lily bug."

"Call me Lily bug one more time Lachlan." She threatened. Curiosity strolled through my veins. What was she going to do? Get pissed and walk away? Good.

"Aw come on Lily bug you used to love that name." I was an asshole. I smiled, still with my eyes closed.

God I wished I hadn't called her Lily bug again. Soft lips crashed against mine. A hiss tore through me. Taking advantage of my surprise, Lily's tongue snuck out and licked the seam of my lips. Holy hell. I was tensed and ready to strike. Radical feelings to wrap my hand in her hair and hold her against my lips assaulted me. I wanted nothing more than to kiss her back and fuck her until the only thing she knew was me. Everything I felt for her came back times ten. I was about to lose control. I felt it, the snap. I couldn't let it happen. She had no idea she was kissing such a monster. A monster who killed his own brother.

I stilled and slowly pushed her back. Eyes opened, looking at hers. They were filled with desire, and anger.

"That won't happen again. You've always been like a little sister to me, Lily. Don't try to fuck that up." I bit out. I was close to snapping. So close.

"Sell your bullshit somewhere else, Lachlan. You may have been pushing me away for the past eight years but I'm not letting you do it anymore." She stood and looked much like Nera. A determined little shit. A warrior.

"Go home, Lily. Go back to your life." I stood up and told her. She looked at me with hate in her eyes. Good.

"I'm not going anywhere, Lachlan." She stood her ground, not moving or running away.

"Things aren't going to end well for you then." I told her straight up before leaving to go back inside. I needed to end this, like now.

We ate dinner as a family and gushed over memories of the past. After dinner, we all sat in the living room and continued to talk and wind down.

"So wanna go with me to Cat's Meow tonight?" I looked at my brother Findley. He wanted me to go to a strip club with him. Why? I felt daggers being nailed into my back and looked at Lily who was sitting close enough to hear what Findley had said. She obviously did not like the thought of me being somewhere like that, even though I had no interest in doing that at all. I agreed. Maybe Lily would see me as the asshole I was and move on.

"Sounds good." I would be asking him why he wanted to go. It wasn't like him to be at a place like that. He gave me a halfhearted smile and looked back at our family. I glanced briefly towards Lily but she had left the room. I sighed to myself. It was better this way. I kept reminding myself that over and over. I didn't see her for the rest of the night and by the time Findley and I left, I still hadn't seen her.

"So why do you want to go to a strip club?" I asked as I plopped down in the passenger seat of his car. He sighed.

"Yeah, Ah figured ye would find it odd." He put the car in gear and started driving towards the club. I kept silent and waited for him to explain. He did. He told me all about this girl named Melissa. She was smart and bright but fell into stripping to pay for her drunk dad and help her mother who already worked two jobs. Fin had fallen head over heels in love and wanted to help her. So he went to the club often and every time he tried to get her to stop, that they would figure it out. I felt bad for him. I vowed in my head that I would check her out. See if she had feelings for him but couldn't quit for the reasons he said or if it was just not mutual.

The Club was quite busy when we walked in. Three girls were dancing on the separate smaller stages. Lonely men on Christmas eve were devouring them with their eyes. I hated being in places like this. All I thought about were how these men were dogs and almost no better than the scum bags who sold girls for their flesh.

"There she is." Fin pointed to a blonde with long legs with cut off shorts and a fancy bra on serving drinks to some guys. One of the men grabbed her ass, obviously harassing her before a bouncer stepped in and told him to back off. I looked at Fin. His jaw was hard and his face held rage. I didn't blame him, if that was my girl that man would be dead by now. She turned to leave the men and her eyes caught Fin's. I didn't even have to talk to her to see she loved my brother back. Her face was filled with love and regret. Something was going on that she couldn't leave this place, but it definitely wasn't because of Fin.

"I'm gonna go talk tae her. Ye'll be ok for like an hour?" He asked, I could see he felt bad bringing me here but maybe he just needed support from his brother. I nodded.

"Yeah, go get her. I'll be alright." I looked around, not really wanting to go sit and watch some girl dance in front of me. I saw a gentleman who looked like some sort of manager and walked over to him.

"I want one of the private rooms, no dancers please. I'll pay for the hour." I told him, he looked at me like I was nuts.

"No girls, eh? Ye sure about that?" He wanted more money.

"Positive." I grabbed a hundred out of my pocket and handed it over. He was still looking at me like I was nuts but took the money and walked me back behind the stage and through a long red hallway then opened a door.

"All yers." He gestured. Once the door was closed I leaned against the door. I was not wanting to sit in that chair in the middle of the room that was probably always covered in cum. The room was designed in black velvet. With a lone, plush chair in the middle facing a glass wall with curtains behind it. I hoped this hour passed quickly.

Thoughts of Lily filtered into my head. Was she pissed I went here? Was she finally going to leave? My thoughts were interrupted when music started playing in the room. That asshole better not have done something he shouldn't have. A streak of light came through the curtain, drawing my attention to the front of the room. A high heeled leg curled around the silk material. Hell, I need to leave.

But as soon as the music kicked it's beat and the curtains open, I was glued to the floor.

Chapter Seven
Lachlan

Long platinum blonde hair flowed down the woman's bare back to her waist. The curves of her hips flared, but were contained in small black shorts that showed perfect round ass cheeks. Legs that flowed towards the floor were lean and looked fucking amazing. Why was I staring at this woman? She was not my Lily. I had to of been seeing things. Imagining her here. The woman slowly bent over, her ass pressed against the glass making my dick shoot up in attention. Fuck. When she came up suddenly her hair flipped back and she turned, showing a sparkling top that covered her breasts and wrapped around her neck.

She moved, grabbing the pole and spinning around it with her hips moving slowly to the beat. I couldn't get a glimpse of her face but her body held me mesmerized. Lily should hate me, I was a bastard and right now was proving it. Years of not caring about women and now that Lily wanted me I found myself hard for another.

The woman lifted herself up the pole and gyrated her hips with the beat then slowly moved down to the floor. Crawling around like a pro then climbed back up the wall, showing me that delectable ass. Which she wiggled back and forth, teasing the hell out of me. I hated I was so attracted to this woman's movements. She was a dancer for sure. I'd seen Lily move enough to recognize it. Then the woman turned and plastered her body to the glassed. Moving like a snake.

I sucked in a breath.

Her face came into focus and I was shocked. My fucking Lily was dancing like she was a goddess of seduction. I should leave, I shouldn't let her see that I'm so affected by her but damn if that snap I knew was coming, happened. I couldn't walk away. Not when she was walking towards me, her hips moving in circles. Her fingers grabbed a handful of my shirt and yanked me closer. Rubbing her body against mine. I knew she felt my cock straining against my jeans because she ground her pelvis against it. She moved backwards and pulled me along. I followed, then she pushed me down in the chair.

"You've been stripping on the side, Lily?" I asked, God I hoped she hadn't. I would have to find some fuckers and burn their eyes out.

"No, but I have been taking vertical fitness classes. Helps to mix it up. Owner is a fan of my ballet." She lowered her body to mine and straddled me. I kept my arms rested on the chair, letting her have control for now.

Her breasts swayed in front of my face as she moved like a snake over my cock.

"Just my body, Lily. That's all I can give you." I told her, she needed to know that was all I would do. She didn't answer me, instead she leaned in and pressed her soft lips to mine. I nipped at her lip and she pulled back.

"I want your body, Lachlan." She paused before getting up. I instantly hated the distance between us. I wanted her body back on mine. Her lips melded to mine.

"But I want your heart more." She whispered softly and walked back behind the glass and the curtains fell. Ending our moment. I let my head fall back on the chair. Fuck my life.

Feeling agitated, I stormed out of the room and went looking for my brother. Fin was at the bar with a short glass of Scotch by the looks of it.

I walked over to him, grabbed more money from my pocket and threw it on the bar.

"We're leaving." I told him. I wanted out of here, I needed quiet, and this place was not quiet.

"Yeah. Let's go." Fin sounded defeated as he started walking towards the door. I followed him out. Leaving the feel of Lily's lips in the dark room, in the back.

I woke up in a panic, my skin was drenched in sweat. My heart was pounding in my chest. I sat up and ran my fingers through my soaked hair. I hadn't had that nightmare in a while. I looked around my room in disgust. Being back home was triggering the nightmares. I fell back against the mattress with a thud. I heard the door knob wiggle and the distinct sound of my door opening.

"Not now, Lily." I knew it was her. No one else bothered me in my room whenever I visited.

"Scoot over." She demanded. I didn't. That was the wrong move with her. She climbed right into my twin sized bed anyways. Her half naked body curled around mine, soothing the pain, but starting to cause another. She didn't say anything and I didn't want to talk. Together we just laid there in that tiny bed. Listening to our hearts beat and our soft breaths. It was calm and peaceful. A peace I hadn't truly had in a long time.

Before I knew it I was fast asleep, the nightmares were gone and all I dreamt about was my starlight. She was guiding me through the land of sleep with her blinding lights of pure goodness.

When the morning sun broke through the window, I felt cold and empty. Lily was no longer in my bed. I hated that I missed her close to me so much. I heard laughter below and thought about just staying in bed for the rest of the day. Wanting to avoid everyone's cheery disposition.

"Lachlan, get yer arse up. Got a surprise for ye." Da's voice boomed through the house. I guess staying in bed was not an option today. Christ being back at home was like being a teenager again, and not the adult I was. I rolled out of bed and stretched. I needed action, my body was aching from lack of movement. I grabbed a t-shirt and put it on before heading to the bathroom to piss. After finishing my business, I walked down the stairs to lots of laughter and voices.

"Hey, there he is." Da gripped me into a hug as soon as I came into the kitchen.

"Look who stopped by." I looked to where he was pointing to see a sight for sore eyes.

"Ye sack of shit!" My Scottish came out of my mouth seeing Wolfe and Nera sitting at my parents table. I walked over and clasped hands with Wolfe. After all these years the rock star and I were damn good friends. It was nice to see. Wolfe's face lit up. He hadn't changed much since the last time I saw him. Same long brown hair tied into a bun on top of his head. His beard was trimmed but still long. His golden eyes held such happiness. Still a big old brute.

"We thought we'd surprise ye." He winked and looked at Nera.

"Little Laoch." I teased. Nera rolled her beautiful eyes. She was such a little beauty. Her Moroccan heritage gave her olive tan skin, and caramel hair a real edge to her look.

"Didn't think you were going to just sit there and not give me a hug did ya?" I scooped up her petite body and hugged her. Nera and I had a bond, one that no one else could understand. I loved her, and after torturing the hell out of her stepparents and step cousin, I was there when her personal hell ended.

"Merry Christmas, Lach." She hugged me back, then went back to her chair. I looked around and other members of my family were walking around, my nieces were screaming and playing with toys they got from Santa. It was very cheerful in this house, just as I thought. The one face that wasn't so cheerful was Lily. Her starlight looked a little dimmed today.

"Morning Lily bug." She flinched at my nickname for her. Maybe I would have to curb that. I didn't want to be a complete dick. Her hair was braided and pulled back behind her head. She was wearing a lavender sweater and black leggings. Her petite feet were tucked into thick wool socks. I wanted to march right over to her and kiss her senseless. When I turned my head back towards our new guests, I saw Nera looking at Lily, then back at me. Wolfe gave me a wink. Aw hell.

"So surprise Christmas present, I must have been a bad boy this year." I teased.
"Wanted to visit Ma, and hang out with tae old gang." He smiled. Well I couldn't fault him there. I was going to call and see if they were around for the holidays.

Ma walked in between us and hugged Wolfe and Nera, probably for the fifth time this morning.

"Now let's get them fed. Breakfast is ready." She kissed them on the check and walked over to the stove to grab a giant plate of pancakes and placed them on the table. Fin and Aiden were the first to tear into them. Beasts they were. But Ma made enough to probably feed the whole neighborhood. Everyone murmured their compliments to the chef as they chewed. Ma always makes great food. My eyes were drawn to Lily every couple of minutes, she wasn't her bright self this morning. Halfway through the meal she excused herself and went up to her room. Concern for her and guilt etched into my soul. I couldn't be with her, but I needed to make things ok between us. I wasn't going to let us fight over something that couldn't be. She wanted my heart, well that boat had long sailed. It's been hers, since I saw her. But I couldn't be hers, and she couldn't be mine. But we could be friends again. Or at least have an understanding.

Once I was finished eating, I excused myself as well and went in search of her. She was indeed sitting on the bed in Grant's old room.

Chapter Eight
Lachlan

"What's going on, Lily?" She looked at me and it must have registered that I didn't call her Lily bug. I walked over and sat down on the bed with her.

"Thank you, for being with me last night." She didn't have to, and I didn't want her to. But she did and it helped. I wasn't a coward that I couldn't admit that. She looked at me and nodded, what for I don't have the slightest clue.

"I heard your scream. I had to do something." Her voice was quiet. What was going on in that head of hers?

"I'm sorry I've been a shit lately. I just." I paused.

"I can't be what you want." She pursed her lips. Wanting to say something but holding it back.

"If I could though, I would try for you." I shouldn't have said it. Words like that can give someone hope. Hope that it will work out in the end.

"Lachlan. I wish I could understand all of this. I get I don't know Lachlan the man but I knew you before the man. I know who you are on the inside. You're a good man. I don't know what you do, or how. I mean I wish I knew, but I know you're not bad. I just wish you'd open up to me." Her words just spilled out of her mouth. I sighed.

"That's where you're wrong Lily. I'm not good." There was no denying it after the things I've done.

"I don't believe you, but I also don't want to argue about it anymore. I'm still going to try for your heart, but I won't push you. I'll wait forever if I have to." I still wished she would give up but it was sort of a truce.

"I won't be a dick anymore." I told her. A little smile broke out on her face. I loved that smile. We stayed silent before a knock on the door jamb caught our attention. Wolfe and Nera were standing there.

"We were going to head over to the fairy pools for a little hike, you guy wanna join?" Nera spoke up. The fairy pools, God I haven't been to them in forever. I looked back at Lily and shrugged.

"Sounds like fun." She piped up. She stood up and held her hand out to me, which I took as she tried to help me up. It was a little comical. I was not a small man at all. Taking pity on her, I stood. Lily went to put her boots on and I went to put on some real clothes.

After dressing in jeans, long sleeve shirt, boots and my gun holstered on my lower back, we walked out towards Wolfe's old truck.

He's had that truck since he was teenager, and even though he has made a shit ton of money from being a rock star, he still would rather drive the old rust bucket.

"I still can't believe you have this truck, Wolfe." Lily hops inside and looks around. We all use to have a blast in this truck.

"Ah could never get rid of her." He rubbed the steering wheel sweetly. Nera scooted in close on the bench front seat and I joined Lily in the back. We looked at each other and went back to looking out the front windshield. We might have called a truce of sorts but things felt a little awkward. I was in uncharted territory. I wanted to be near her, but not give her any hope that there would be more.

I had a few more days left before I had to go on a mission, and I wasn't sure what I was going to do after that. Would I go back to being the lone wolf I was, or spend more time with my friends and family?

"So how long are you guys here for?" I asked the couple up front. Nera answered me while Wolfe got the truck on a roll towards the pools.

"We didn't really have any set plans. I know we have to be in New York in a two months for a concert. Wolfe's got a busy tour schedule." She did something to him that made him squirm a little. I shook my head, and to think she had fought this. The rest of the thirty-minute drive we talked about Wolfe's music tours, and the madness. They talked about the craziness that happened at a scavenger hunt last Halloween at Edinburgh castle. Sounded like their lives were amazing. I was truly happy for them. We pulled into the parking lot and found it empty.

Everyone was probably spending their Christmas with their families.

"I haven't been here since we were teens." Lily looked excited as she got out of the car.

"Same here." I told her. She looked at me and smiled. Maybe we could get past the awkwardness. Nera was practically jumping with excitement as she walked around the back of the truck, looking around.

"I'm gonna go pee. Be right back!" She smiled and turned towards the bathrooms. Lily ran over to her.

"I better go too!" She said to us. I shook my head. Women, always going to the bathroom together. I looked around at the black mountains and took a breath. There really wasn't another place like home.

"Still fighting it aren't ye? Ah still don't see why." Wolfe walked up and stood beside me.

"You know it won't work." I was tired of going over this with everyone.

"She's tougher than she looks ye know. If anyone could be tae woman for ye. It would be her. Always thought ye two would end up together. Trust me, Lachlan. Love is the one thing that keeps away the demons." I didn't answer, I knew by watching him and Nera, that it had worked for them. I turned at the sound of Lily laughing.

What if I gave into my love for Lily and it consumed us both? I was dark, and she was light. My darkness would eventually snuff hers out.

The feelings that once again swept over me were the reasons I stayed away from her for so long. It was a feeling of hopelessness, and devastation. I felt my phone buzz in my pocket and pulled it out.

It was an email for my next mission. Shit has taken a turn up shits creek and I was needed sooner. Tomorrow.

I looked up at Lily and decided to enjoy the rest of the day with her and my friends. I wasn't sure I would be back after tonight. My life was never tethered. I went where my missions took me.

"You guys ready?" Nera asked, her arm laced with Lily's.

"Let's go little Laoch." I winked at her and together we walked down the path to the first pool.

Chapter Nine
Lily

Ever since Nera and I came out of the bathroom, Lachlan had seemed off. Like something got into his head. He wasn't one hundred percent himself, although I was coming to find out the man was not like the boy I knew. He was still in there, but this man was different. He was torn, and even dangerous. I could feel it coming off of him in vibes and I didn't know why. He was untouchable with that wall wrapped around his soul so tight.

I took in the scenery of the pools but my mind was all on him. He acted like everything was ok on the outside, but we weren't fooled. Nera whipped out a camera and started snapping pictures. They were adorable to watch together, taking selfies and laughing at each other's stupid grins.

"Get over here. Let's all get in the picture!" Nera called out. I looked over at Lachlan who had just picked up a stone from the beneath the water. He looked up and started walking over to them, I joined the group.

Together we smushed our faces together and Nera tried to hold her petite arms out far enough to take a selfie of us. Poor girl, like me we were kinda little, especially compared to the two brute-like men at our sides. I heard both Lachlan and Wolfe chuckle at her struggle before Wolfe stepped in.

"Give it." He demanded and she handed it over easily.

"Give it yer best." He said and I smiled. It wasn't my full smile but it would do. I was enjoying our time together, but I couldn't fully let go while I knew something was off with Lachlan. I tried though. I let myself get distracted in the scenery for a few moments. The air was a little crisp, but the grass was green and the pools were always something like out of a fairytale. Waterfalls, peaceful sounds, wind rustling around.

Then before I knew it, we were on our way back to Lachlan's parents' house and saying bye to Nera and Wolfe. They would be around, and I promised Nera that we would get together while they were here before they departed. I went straight up to the bedroom and grabbed my stuff for a shower. I needed to think. I didn't know what to do about Lachlan. I threw it out there. I've tried to get him to see we could be good together but there has to be something else happening. I walked into the bathroom and turned on the water. As I got in, I wondered about what I was going to do.

    I smacked my hand against the tile of the shower. I was so frustrated. I could see it in his eyes. He wanted me. He might even love me. He might not know that I noticed his glances my way but when he looked at me I saw past the mask he tried to put on. I saw pain, and longing.

    I wanted his lips on mine again. I wanted his touch, but dammit I wanted all of him.

    I finished my shower and dried off.

    Once I was dressed, I went back downstairs to see everyone comfortably sitting in the living room. Aiden and Lachlan were playing some board game. Their parents were talking to Fin and laughing. It was a beautiful scene. I missed my mom.

    She died a year ago from breast cancer. It was rough, Lance really helped me through the tough moments. But I dedicated the past year of dance to her. I've been traveling and dancing my heart out for her. My home was where my main stage was.

"Lily, come join us honey." Lachlan's mom waved me over. I smiled at her and joined them while they talked about fun things that were happening at the car shop. I was impressed with all the changes they had made. Time seemed to have stayed still at this house. Everyone was going on with their lives. Being happy, while I was frustrated to hell. Not to mention the more I kept sneaking glances at Lachlan, the hotter I was getting in my leggings.

I couldn't explain it. He was just wearing jeans, boots, and a long sleeve shirt. Nothing crazy. But it hugged his hard muscles. His brown hair was a little messy like he had been running his fingers through it. I wanted to do that.

As if he sensed me watching him, he looked my way and he had a hard look in his eyes. He smiled at his little brother and got up to come over to our little conversation.

"Hey ma. I've got to head out tonight but I'll be back for Roderick's party." His mom wasn't too happy about it but she never got mad at him for anything. Why did he have to leave? They just accepted this without knowing where he was going?

"Ok dear, be safe." He kissed her cheek and shook hands with his dad before heading upstairs. Feeling all sorts of emotions, I excused myself and followed after him. I wasn't sure what I was going to say, but I had to do something. I felt like he was just saying he would be back but didn't really mean it. If I didn't do something, he would be gone and I might not every get the chance again. I opened the door gently to his room and saw him packing what little belongings he had into a small bag.

"You're leaving?" He turned towards me, that mask still on one hundred percent.

"Yep, got shit I gotta do."

"Are you really coming back?" I took a step closer. His eyes swept down my legs and back up to my eyes. The mask slipped a tiny bit.

"I don't know." His answer was honest. I felt the tiniest hint of relief that what he said was true, but then the fear spiked back in my blood. I might not ever see him again. He could run off this time and that would be it. I took another step closer.

"Don't shut me out this time." I closed the distance between us and looking into his eyes, hopefully conveying my feelings in that look.

"Lily." His voice sounded exasperated. He was tired of this game. I was too. I didn't want him to fight me anymore.

"I'm not going to let you." My hands reached out and touched his chest. I wanted a hiss, or some sort of reaction from him, something to see that when we touched I meant something. That his heart raced and his body heated like mine did.

"You don't have a say, Lily." The mask was slipping. His face was hardening; his beautiful sharp jaw was tensing. He was fighting this. So hard. My hands moved over his abs and up his pecs. He'd grown so much since I'd last saw him. He was all man, every last lickable inch of him.

"I'm staking my say." I leaned in close, and he froze. I was getting somewhere in there. Every move made a difference. Our eyes were locked on one another's. His pleading with me to leave, mine begging for him to give up. I moved the last bit and pressed my body against his. My hands moved up and traced his tense jaw. It slackened a little and his lips parted ever so slightly. There was no need for words right now. Words might even ruin all this distance I'd crossed.

No, we needed to communicate without the use of words. My exploring hands moved to the base of his head, teasing the hairs there. I felt his body tremor softly.

Taking a leap of faith, I raised up onto my toes and pressed my lips to his. He didn't move.

I needed his mask to fall. I needed him. I was aching, and alone.

"Lachlan." I moaned. My hands gripped those sensitive hairs. The hiss I'd wanted earlier came through his lips. I nipped at his parted lower lip.

"I need you." I pleaded on breathless groan. I was burning, and by the vibes that were coming off of him, he was to. Only he was still fighting it.

I tried again to get him to kiss me. My tongue flicked his lips and it happened.

His mouth molded to mine. His hands went to my hips, he pressed me against his cock and I groaned. I'd wanted him for so long, every man I'd ever had never matched to him.

My leg lifted trying to get a better angle on his cock. Something animalistic came from his chest as he gripped behind my legs and hoisted me up, my legs wrapped around him and I was right where I wanted to be.

He stood there holding me in the middle of the room. Our lips moved, and tongues tangled. The dam was broken and I was never going back. I would do whatever it took to have him in my life. Not just as my lover, but my future, my home.

Chapter Ten
Lily

He turned and I was suddenly pressed between a hard surface and his hard body. It was heaven. I knew Lachlan wouldn't be the type of man to make love to you sweetly in the missionary position every night. No, Lachlan was the type of man to dominate you. Make you whimper and cry for every morsel of his touch. He would throw everything he had into your needs. All danger meshing with pure uninhibited passion. His hips thrust forward and my head fell back. His mouth latched onto my neck and his hands went straight to my breasts. I was pinned to the wall by his cock and I wanted nothing more than to be nailed in permanently.

"You want my cock don't you sweet Starlight?" He pistoned his hips back and forth slowly. He called me Starlight. That was something new.

"I bet you're soaking wet for this cock right now, the very smell of it is making me want to part that sweet, pink flesh and fuck it till it's raw. You'll feel me for days." He groaned at his own words. I knew it. Lachlan was not a sweet words and hearts man. I knew what I was getting and I was loving every second of it.

"But I'm not going to fuck you tonight, Starlight. I'm not going to take you with my family laughing downstairs. I want you to myself, no one else is privileged to hear your cries."

I shook my head no. It may make me a total slut to say that but I didn't care one single bit. I just wanted him. I was about to say something but then his lips were back on mine. His kiss was consuming my every thought. I was mindless, only my body's needs prevailed.

We touched, and we moved together but no one was finding release tonight.

After a few minutes, our kisses slowed and our hands were still. I knew we'd had a big change in our relationship, something snapped. But how far that change went, I didn't know.

"I'll come back Lily. But I still don't promise forever." His forehead touched mine as he whispered towards me. I wanted forever, but I would be patient. In time it would come. There was no fighting it after what just happened.

"Ok." I was giving in too. I was having faith that things would work out. We would make it work.

"Do you know when you'll be back?" I was hoping it wouldn't be a long trip. And I knew asking him where he was going and what he would be doing was pointless.

"In a few days." My relief was audible. We just stayed there, me pinned to the wall, looking at each other. Taking the sight in. Memorizing.

"You're so beautiful, always have been." He stated. I know I felt blush coat my cheeks. I always thought I looked like a weird alien with my platinum blonde hair and purple eyes. I laid my head down on his shoulder and he walked us to his bed with me still straddling his waist. He sat down and wrapped his arms around me. He was so solid, I felt so safe surrounded by him.

To lighten the tension Lachlan chose the moment to head down memory lane.

"I used to think about you when we were teens a lot. What it would be like to have you in my arms like this. Have you in my bed." He admitted.

"Why didn't you say anything?" If he had, I would have thrown my virginity and my heart at him years ago. So many things could have been different. He sighed and his head fell to my shoulder.

"I was like a big brother to you. I didn't want to change the dynamic of our relationship and lose you." While I could understand that, I don't think it would have.

"And then you ended up losing me anyways." By choice. I wanted to add that at the end of my statement, but we both knew it was his choice to disappear.

"I did." He sounded devastated. I wish I knew everything that was going on in his head. Lighten the burden that weighed him down so heavily.

But alas, our time was up. His phone that was on the bed behind him buzzed. He pulled back to check in and then set me on the bed next to him.

"I've gotta go." He looked at his phone then back at me. I was sad, but he said he'd be back so I was going to trust that.

"Be safe." I told him with a halfhearted smile. He leaned in and pressed a sweet kiss to my lips.

He zipped up his bag and stood. He didn't say anything else before he left the room but that last kiss was everything he could have said and more. He was trying. I laid back on his bed and relished in his smell that came off the pillow. Things were different, and when he came back, things were going to change even more. I just knew it.

Chapter Eleven
Lachlan

I was losing blood, and things were not looking good.

"Good work, money will be transferred immediately." The FBI agent walked off to his SUV.

I waited until the SUV drove away before looking at my patch job. It hurt like hell to lift my shirt to see the wound. My mission was successful, but I didn't come out of it unscathed. One of the asshats got me with a knife to the side. I did what I could and stitched it up myself but it looked like I was going to have to go to the hospital.

Quickly, I hopped into my unmarked black car and drove to the nearest emergency room. I felt my head getting light, and my vision started to blur around the edges.

Shit.

I parked in the valet line and handed the man the keys. I couldn't give a shit what happened to it. It wasn't even mine. I walked up to the front desk calmly, and gripped the edge of the desk for support. My side was throbbing and I felt like I was going under.

"I got stabbed." I told her before my vision went black.

* * *

It had been three weeks since I'd blacked out in the emergency room.

Three weeks since I'd left Lily sitting on my bed.

I needed blood and surgery. The knife had gone deeper than I'd thought, but I'd live to kill another day.

I had wanted to call Lily, apologize for not coming back to Scotland. But I couldn't, not yet. I needed to heal, I needed to think. I wasn't ready to walk away from her again, but shit like this only made me think about how my life was too dangerous.

I could leave on missions and never come back. Or exactly like what happened where I would be hit and wouldn't be back for days. She would worry, and if something ever happened it would kill her light. I couldn't do that to her, but dammit to hell if I could stay away from her now. I was fucked. Pure and simple.

As I walked towards the building that housed a dance studio inside, I became nervous. Not an emotion I was used to. Once my wound was healed most of the way. I hopped on a plane and hauled ass home. Hoping she'd still be there. Thoughts were running through my head on my travels.

What if she gave up and left?

What if she hadn't and was still waiting?

Would she be pissed at me for not coming back as soon as I said?

It wasn't like I was going to tell her what exactly happened. I couldn't lay that on her without explaining anything else.

But when I touched down, I called Ma and apologized. She understood, even though she didn't know what exactly I did but I knew she knew something. Just not what.

She told me not so subtly that Lily was still around and had started going to the local college to dance on their stage to practice. Thrilled to have a famous dancer around, they let her use it as her own personal studio. She also didn't miss the chance to tell me I needed to sweep her off her feet before someone else did.

I opened the door and strolled towards the stage where I was told she would be. I had so many things to say but when I walked into the room all of those words died in my throat.

She was rolling on the ground. The purple shirt she was wearing was cut short and showing her toned stomach. She as wearing black shorts and leg warmers. My eyes drank her in like she was a divine angel to behold.

I sat in the chair closest to the back, in the darkness and watched her give her soul to her craft. Her love of dancing.

The music was intense, a feminine voice filled the room.

Her arms moved, and her head rolled. She rose up only to fall down again. Like something was pulling her down, not allowing her to see the sun again.

As the song grew in intensity she twirled, and flipped across the stage like she was the strong voice itself. Her movements were graceful but sharp. Almost like she was in battle. Fighting to breathe, fighting to continue on.

I hadn't watched her dance since that one night years ago when I finally walked away from her, never to see her again. Didn't work out the way I had hoped. Now I was having trouble staying away. Her lips beckoned me, and thoughts of her touch were going to drive me mad. Those same hands traveled over her own body. I felt my dick stirring from watching her dance. She always threw every cell of her being into dancing. I admired it and damn, if I didn't find it attractive as hell right now. Until I saw her face when the song came to a close. That face was of a woman who was hurting.

    I was hurting her, the only girl who I've cared about more than my own life. I stood and walked towards her. Last time I did the opposite and walked out the door, but not this time. I still didn't really know what the hell I was doing with her, but this was something I could control.

    She fell to the ground on the last note. The way she collapsed broke my heart. Her dancing always did draw out many emotions from me. And right now I was feeling hate for my life. Hate that I was doing this to her. I should leave. God I should just let her hurt right now, and get over it later. Fuck it.

    "Lily" I said aloud, alerting her that I was here. Her head snapped up so hard I was afraid she would get whiplash.

"Lachlan?" She squinted through the lights to the dark room I was in. I kept myself from hauling ass to her only because I didn't know how she was feeling right now from seeing me. When I finally started making my ascent up the stairs, I noticed her body locked up. Not a good sign.

"That was amazing." I gave her a little smile. I neared her and when I was finally maybe two feet away I crouched down, ignoring the slight twinge in my side. She hadn't said anything. I took a deep breath and said what I could.

"I'm sorry. Shit like this happens in my life, but I did come back." She didn't really know me much anymore but to me that was a big deal. I came back for her, even though I shouldn't have. I waited and watched her as she processed my apology and looked me over. I wanted to say so much more. That I loved her, that she was the very air I breathed, and I never wanted to leave her. But of course I was a shithead and wouldn't.

The tension between us was electric. It gave me the same tingles in my skin like I would get right before I dove into mission. Anticipation with a hint of fear.

"You came back." She murmured. I wasn't prepared when she launched herself at me, so when she did we went to the ground. I was shocked as shit when her lips crushed against mine. She wasn't running. She didn't hate me.

Chapter Twelve
Lachlan

Once the shock was done running through my veins, I gave fully into her kiss. Fuck, did I miss her lips. Her smell. Hell I just straight missed her. My arms wrapped her in a vice above me.

When her tongue snaked out and touched mine, I growled and flipped us so she was now on bottom and I loomed over her. I was a dominant man, a real caveman. She gasped and I fought for control to not fuck her on the damn lit up stage. Her nails scratched my back and a hiss came from my throat.

"Lily, unless you want to be fucked on this stage where anyone could see us then I suggest we cool it." I warned her, but damn it if she didn't push me to my limits. Her little hips lifted and started rotating against my cock.

"Damn it, Lily." It was my last warning. I was a bastard for even thinking of doing what was racing through my mind. I was so consumed by my thoughts of keeping it in my pants, that I hadn't noticed her sneaky hand moved around my waist and gripped my cock.

Fuck that control. It snapped. I lost it. I'd wanted her for too damn long and if she was willing to play with fire than we would both burn in the flames of this delicious sin.

She was on the same track mind as me while her hand worked the button of my jeans, unleashing me, touching my cock skin to skin.

I gripped her shorts and pulled them down swiftly.

God she was beautiful, Purple shirt, sweat matted hair, and leg warmers.

So many thoughts were running through my head, but none of them were smart. I imagined this moment since I was a teen. Nothing could compare. I wished we were in a bed or something sweet. She deserved that. She must have seen the hesitation in my eyes, then wrapped her legs around me, lining us up. I felt her heat caressing me. Screw being good.

I rubbed my cock up and down her slit, making sure she was ready. As soon as I found her soaking, I plunged in. My head rolled and she gasped. Holy hell, she was made for me.

"Lachlan, look at me." My head snapped to hers. She was glowing, and needy.

The caveman in me thought only one thing. Satisfy my woman.

I braced my arms around her head and moved with a passion of ten years in the making.

Her hands gripped my back while she held on for her life. I was not taking it nice and slow. No fuckin way. This was what you got with me, I was rough, and hard. Her moans only fueled my desire, making me crazy with need for her. She wiggled and I felt her body start to tense. Our eyes never swayed, we were completely in this together. Body, mind, and soul in that moment, I almost gave into the thoughts of a future I never wanted. With her amethyst eyes playing hostage with mine, I felt her hope. The love that we could have. I almost said it. It was on the tip of my tongue. To try and give us what we truly wanted, but I held those words back. Her eyes closed briefly and I popped her clit.

"Eyes" Her eyes were wide from my surprising pop but they were back on me. Her legs tightened and her pussy started to quiver. She was about to explode. I felt the tingles start in my balls, and it started to move up my spine.

"Starlight, come for me baby." I gritted my teeth; I would not come yet. She bit her lip as if she was holding back too. Yeah right, like I was going to let that happen. I switched angles and lifted her leg up onto my shoulder. Three thrusts and she was done. Her cries echoed on the stage.

The look of the pure ecstasy in her eyes did me in. I came harder than I've ever had before. I rode through the pleasure and when I was done, I kissed my girl.

"No going back Lachlan, ok?" She whispered to me, and I nodded. It was all I could do. I looked around and noticed there was a little line of light from one of the doors in the back. Shit. Not even thirty seconds later the door closed.

I pulled out, stood while lifting Lily up into my arms. I needed her to have some privacy. Someone had just watched us fuck. I didn't truly give a shit, but I wanted her to feel safe.

"Yikes, I guess we got caught." She giggled as I set her down behind the curtains.

"Probably some punk kid." I tucked myself back in my pants and did up my zipper.

She cleaned herself up with her panties and put her shorts on. Oh shit.

"Shit, Lily I didn't use a condom." I was a little freaked.

"It's ok, I'm on the pill and I'm clean. You?" She looked at me.

"I'm good." I wasn't sure if we were about to have the past lovers talk. If so, she was probably going to be shocked. It had been a long time since I'd gotten laid. After I walked away from her years ago, I tried to forget about her and screw other women, but after a while I realized nothing would be right but her. Call it my penance for all of my sins, not only could I not have the girl I wanted, but I would not have any other pussy too.

"You ok?" I needed to know she wasn't regretting what we did. She had a faint blush on her face but other than that all she looked was satisfied.

"Yeah, I just feel like a noodle." She smiled and I brought her into my arms. She squeezed me gently, which hurt my side but I didn't show it.

"Sorry I didn't take you in a bed or do sweet shit for our first time." I felt like a bastard for taking her out in a public place where obviously people could watch. She looked up at me and I was curious what she was thinking.

"I like no beds with you." She reached up and brought my lips down to hers. How the hell was I not going to get used to this?

Her kiss seared my soul. It was almost too much that I had to pull away.

"Can we go back to my place and talk?" She asked and I nodded.

"You have a place?" I guess she wouldn't want to stay with my parents for any long length of time. She started walking and I followed her to a room behind the stage where her stuff was in a locker.

"Yep. But we can talk about it when we get there." She grabbed her small purse and walked out a side door. The parking lot only had a few cars in it, and she headed straight for a little white Mini Cooper. How cute.

"I'll grab my SUV and follow you." I grabbed her by the arm and pulled her in for a kiss, before walking towards my ride.

Keeping my eyes on my surroundings was a habit I'd picked up over time. You never knew when someone was watching and not your friend. Nothing looked out of order besides a man in slacks with a brief case, probably a teacher getting into his car, and then there were two guys making out by their car. I wasn't into that, but good for them.

After unlocking the Tahoe, I hopped in and saw that Lily's little white mini was waiting for me. She drove ahead and I followed her all the way to some bright colored apartments by the loch. She pulled into a spot in front of the light blue one.

"Interesting choice." I commented as we got out of our cars. She looked at the building and smiled.

"I always wanted to live here growing up. A view on the loch, it's pretty." She gestured for us to walk towards her place.

"Ladies first." I one hundred percent would admit that I stared at her ass as she waltzed up to her door. 2B. She fiddled with her keys and opened the door. Her apartment was tidy, and calm. Light colors and one picture of a dancer in the living room, but other than that It seemed impersonal.

"When did you move here?" I was anxious to get the talking out of the way. She set her purse down and walked into what I assumed was her bedroom. Talking to me while I stayed standing in her living room.

"About a week after you left. I didn't want to hang around your parents until you came back. So I found this place, the owners are touring the world. Bucket listers. They wanted someone to take care of the place while they were gone, and watch after Lola." Sure enough after she said that a cat ran out from behind the couch and into the room Lily was in. Sounded like she had gotten a good deal.

Chapter Thirteen
Lachlan

"Ok, I feel better." She walked out wearing tight yoga pants, and a big, plain, blue shirt tied in a knot at her hip. Her hair was still a mess, but it worked. She sat on the small couch and patted the cushion next to her for me to sit. I did.

"I'm mad you didn't come back in a few days like you said." I started to say something but she held her hand out stopping me.

"But you came back and that says something. Something big. So, obviously I've had a lot of time to think. If we are really going to try for anything together, we have to figure out what we need from each other." She kept going. I remember she used to do stuff like this back in the day. Once she had something on her mind, don't try to get in a word until she was done. It was pointless.

"I need you to somehow communicate to me that you're ok. Or something, just somehow let me know that you're alive. Text me, email, call, fax me, or send a bloody pigeon. Anything. I can deal as long as you can give me that." I thought over her words, could I do that?

"I can't do it every day. It might be a few." Sometimes I was completely off the radar for some missions.

"Ok, how about every Sunday. You let me know you're alive." She was negotiating. I found it cute.

"OK." I agreed.

"Alright, now. I have no clue what you do for a living, and I'm pretty sure you won't tell me if I asked. But can you tell me if it is dangerous work?" I chewed over the thought of lying but if I didn't have to, then I shouldn't.

"Yes." She took a few breaths after my answer. This was where whatever we were attempting to have would get complicated.

"Do you work with people or alone?" She wanted to know more.

"Alone."

"Should I be worried about my safety?" She seemed a little nervous, I wished she hadn't asked that question. Truly.

"From me, no. From being with me, yes. But I won't let anything happen to you." I vowed, but somewhere inside me I knew it wasn't something I should be saying. I did dirty work. I've made enemies. People who would try to hurt me. I distanced myself from anyone who could be used against me. She seemed to ponder that information a little longer.

"How long were you going to wait?" I inquired. It was something that was running through my mind the whole time. Was she about to pack up and leave tomorrow? I doubt she would have waited for my ass for a year. Hell, I wouldn't want her to do that. She turned towards me and ran her fingers along my jaw line. It was an emotional touch.

"As long as it took for you to come back to me." Her voice was low but strong. So strong. I loved and hated her words in the same sentence.

"Dammit Lily. You shouldn't feel this way." I stood. I didn't know how to feel about her staying. Happy? Pissed? Indifferent? I started pacing.

"I'm not fucking good for you. I should have stayed away. You could go live a happy life without me dragging you down into my darkness." My hands ran down my face in frustration. I looked at her to see her watching me curiously.

"I can't do this, Lily. We have a past, and I can't allow anything to fuck up your life, including me being in it." I was pushing her away. It was the right thing. I couldn't have her waiting for me all the time. What if I never came back? She would be crushed. I felt defeated and whatever the hell we were trying for was gone. I felt like my normal self. The self-loathing killer. Lily was staring at me blankly. No emotions or anything. Maybe this was a good thing then.

Until she jumped up and pushed me back.

"Don't you dare do this right now. How about instead of..."

Push.

"You deciding what's best for me in my life."

Push.

"You let me in on the decision. If I want to go down into your darkness as you put it, then that's my fucking choice."

She tried to push me again but I grabbed her wrists. I was done with that shit.

"You done?" I asked her, it was my turn. Would I open up and tell her everything? No. But maybe she needed a tiny eye opener that she should run far away from me.

Chapter Fourteen
Lily

I was so furious, and strangely turned on. Fighting with him was making every nerve in my body come alive. Something was wrong with me.

I didn't say anything as he constrained my wrists and stared down at me with those eyes that hinted to the danger inside him. I wanted to know that side. I wanted to know everything about him, inside and out. He brought my hands down to my sides and let go. He gripped the bottom of his shirt and lifted it up and over his head. Displaying one hell of a torso. A delicious torso that I wanted to worship. Except.

My hand went up to my lips to cover my gasp.

"Yeah Lily, soak it in. The reason I didn't come back was because I got stabbed. Lost a lot of blood and had to go to the hospital." He said it like he was trying to scare me with this revelation. It kind of did. But I already suspected things like this could happen. He said he saved me from my captives, he couldn't have done that if he wasn't into some seriously dangerous stuff.

My fingers left my mouth, bee lining to touch the puckered skin where he must have been stitched. His ab muscles tightened when my fingers met his flesh. It was rough. It had to of hurt. My eyes scanned past his gloriously rippled stomach in search of more. There were a few scars here and there. Another puckered scar on his right shoulder. Gun shot? I wish I could have been there to help take care of him.

"Yeah, that's what I thought. It's too much to handle." He started to put his shirt back on but I gripped it from him and threw in on the floor.

"Did I fucking say that?" God he was being such an ass.

"I can see it on your face." He spat.

"No, you wanna know what I'm thinking, besides that you're being an asshole." He just stared at me, not so patiently waiting.

"I was thinking I wish I was there. I could have taken care of you. Been there for you." I moved closer and pressed a kiss to the scar on his shoulder. I moved to a smaller scar and kept talking, but against his hot skin.

"This doesn't scare me away, Lachlan. I don't know what you do, but I know it's dangerous. I get it. I want to be your home base. Your serenity. I want to help you heal from these mortal wounds." I meant every word. I was not letting him go, no matter what.

"What's wrong with you? Why would you want to willingly be a part of my world?" His voice was low; he was losing his battle of trying to push me away.

"I love you, Lachlan. I always have." I kissed his nipple, swirling my tongue around it. I waited for him to throw a little hissy fit at my admission but I wasn't one to run away from my feelings, unlike a tall, dark and handsome Scot. His body froze and I was a little worried I broke him with my words. He took a step back, out of my reach. He looked at me like I had five heads. I was confused. Wasn't he supposed to admit he loved me back and we would be ok?

Without even grabbing his shirt, he walked right to the door and left. I just stared at the door, trying to understand what just happened. He left?

He left? After I just told him I loved him. That wasn't how that was supposed to go. I went to the couch and sat down. Emotions started to smother me. What if I just made a huge mistake?

"Oh god." I whispered to the empty apartment. I fucked up, I pushed him too hard. My eyes started to water when I heard the door shut. I kept my head down, if it was him I didn't want to see anything on his face. I felt like a fool for putting my heart out there. God, besides fucking on the stage we were still like strangers.

"Lily, what did Ah tell ye about locking that damn door." Wolfe walked into the room with Nera following behind him. My heart sank a little more, Lachlan really left.

I forgot they said they were coming over for an early dinner. I looked up and shrugged. They set a few bags on the table and came over to me.

"We saw Lachlan leave the apartment. Everything ok?" Nera sat down to the right of me on the couch while Wolfe plopped down in the chair to the left of me.

I shook my head.

"I pushed him too hard." I admitted, I felt horrible. He wasn't ready to hear how I felt about him, now I could have lost him forever.
"He'll bounce back." Wolfe commented but I didn't feel confident about that.

"Why do you think you pushed him away?" Nera probed. I looked at her, she was genuinely concerned. Maybe it was a girl thing, because when I looked at Wolfe he didn't seem the least bit worried about me upsetting Lachlan.

"I told him I loved him, after he tried to end whatever it was we were becoming." I was such a fool.

"Hmm, I wouldn't worry too much, it was obvious..."

"Nera." Wolfe coughed, interrupting what she was going to say. I looked at him and he tried to shrug it off. What was going on right now? I was about to answer when the door opened again. My eyebrows furrowed in confusion.

Lachlan strode through the door, he walked in not paying any attention to Wolfe or Nera sitting there. Nera was gaping at his naked torso. Couldn't say I blamed her, even with him looking pissed and on a mission it was hard not to appreciate that display of sexiness.

"Aye, put yer shirt on ye fool." Wolfe was shaking his head at us women.

"Lachlan?" I wanted to apologize. I wanted to tell him I wished I could turn back time and not tell him how I felt just yet. But I didn't have that chance. He picked me up and threw me over his shoulder and walked away from the living room and into the bedroom.

I heard a chuckle from behind us before he closed the door to my room.

"Lachlan, put me down." I smacked his very nice behind. He tossed me down on the bed and covered my body with his. I was officially confused.

"Tell me again." He murmured as he started kissing my neck.

Well, helloo. This was not at all what I was thinking was going to happen. It felt so good. I couldn't control my hands from touching them. "Tell you what again?" I whimpered.

"You know what." He growled.

"I love you." Despite being a little scared at saying it out loud, I took that leap of faith that uttering those words was what he wanted from me.

"You're mine." His lips smashed against mine with uninhibited passion. I was still shocked by everything that was happening right now. Just a minute ago, I was about to cry my eyes out and now I have Lachlan attached to my lips, trying to get inside. And as much as I wanted that, I needed some verbal action, we needed to talk.

"Lachlan, stop." I moaned when he nipped at my lower lip. He pulled back slowly and looked at me, obviously wondering why I stopped him.

"You have to explain what just happened, I told you I loved you." His eyes closed briefly at those words.

"Then you stormed off. Now you're back and mauling me." His hand reached up and moved along my hair line, it was such a sweet gesture.

"Those words coming from your sweet mouth was something I'd never wanted to hear, but always did crave to hear."

He said what?

"I dreamed of for so long, wanting to have you in my arms, but punishing myself for the sins I've done by staying away. I could never deserve you. I'm still a bad man, but once you said those words I had to leave to take it in. I hated myself just knowing that I couldn't just walk away anymore. You've always had my heart, even if you didn't know. Now I have yours, and it's pure and clean. I can't destroy it now that it's mine."

I had no words. Tears started to fall down my cheeks. He hadn't said I love you, but he said I've had his heart.

"Lachlan." I was about to say more when a banging on the door cut me off. I looked over to it wondering if it was broken.

"Get yer arses out here, there will be time for fucking later." Wolfe bellowed. I started giggling when I heard a distinct smack noise. Nera so owned him. I gazed back at Lachlan to see him staring at me.

"Yer laugh soothes me." His Scottish accent came out just a little bit there. I wondered why he hid it.

"We better get out there." I tried to push him off but he wouldn't budge.

"Come on you big brute. Let's go see our friends." He still didn't get off me but leaned down and kissed me instead. This kiss was unlike the one before, this was something bigger. I didn't know what but it just felt important. When he pulled back, I was sure there were stars in my eyes.

"Come on, you can quit mauling me now." He teased and got off me real quick. I chased after him but he ran out the door and was putting on his shirt when I reached him. He ducked out of the lite push I was going to give him but then wrapped his arms around me and held me like he won the moon.

Chapter Fifteen
Lily

"Told ye." Wolfe winked and Nera was beaming at us. Well Lachlan did bounce back very quickly.

"So, what are you lot doing here?" The man behind me spoke up.

"We were going to have dinner. Then I don't know. Did we have any more plans?" She looked at Wolfe who proceeded to shrug. He was so shruggy today. I answered for him.

"Nope, we were just going to hang out and drink a little." I untangled myself from my love and Nera and I got to work on unloading everything from the bags for dinner.

"I'm glad it worked out between you two." Nera whispered to me while grabbing a frying pan from the cabinet below. The apartment was pretty open so it was nice to be in the kitchen but still be part of the happenings in the living room. So Lachlan and Wolfe could be heard talking about a car that Wolfe had hired Fin to bring back to life.

"Me too. It's a dream come true." I admitted to her. We started cooking chili and getting all the chips, sour cream, and cheese ready to go. It took about an hour and then we all dug in. Every once in a while Lachlan would give me a look that said he would rather be eating me than the chili, which only made me think of how amazing he had felt between my legs.

"Man, I'm stuffed." Nera relaxed back into the wooden chair. She was so petite but man could she knock back some food. Wolfe told me she didn't get to experience many choices of food when she was younger so she took advantage of it now.

"You killed it, Laoch." Lachlan teased her. They had such a strange relationship, I wish I understood it more.

"Shh." She bit out with a smile.

"So Lily, when is yer next show?" Wolfe asked. Over the years, he had actually come to a couple of my shows if he was in town. I traveled all over the world, doing different shows. I had gone to Julliard after high school and excelled at all my classes. I got accepted into the best dance companies there were, and I had been loving every minute of it.

"I don't have any planned for a couple of months actually. After what happened, I kind of wanted take a break." To be honest I sort of had a little PTSD from being taken. While I don't remember it completely, I still was a little nervous that someone was out to grab me again.

"I have a good therapist if you need someone to talk to." Nera stated, maybe that would be a good idea.

"I might do that, but I think I'll feel better after tomorrow." I winked at her.

"What's tomorrow?" Lachlan asked, looking between the two of us.

"Tired of tae lassies in mah life gittin kidnapped. Signed them up for self-defense class tomorrow." Wolfe answered. He was pretty adamant about us learned the basics. He had mentioned it when we were on the phone before I flew out here and I was looking forward to it actually.

"Good plan." Lachlan agreed. It was nice hanging out with everyone like this. I really hoped this calm would last, but something in the back of my head told me it was just a calm before the storm. We ended up watching the highland games that was on TV. Wolfe and Nera, who were snuggled up together on the recliner, talked about how much fun they had at the big games when they went. It was that moment Wolfe got outed to Nera as Rock God. I was happy for them. Lachlan sat beside me on the couch and I cuddled close.

    I didn't really know when I dozed off, but I heard Nera and Wolfe say bye, then I was lifted into the air and Lachlan was carrying me to the bedroom. I was so tired. Seeing him again and the stage sex, followed by everything else had just wiped me. He laid me down and took off most of his clothes before jumping into bed with me. I wish I had the energy to enjoy his body in bed with mine, but as his arms wrapped around me I passed out.

    Man I had one hell of a dream. Sex with Lachlan, then dancing naked in front of a huge audience, and someone taking me and throwing me in a dark room.

    I woke up startled and looked around. Lachlan was still asleep next to me. Thank God. I took a few breaths to help calm my heart, that dream was crazy. Maybe I really did need to give Nera's therapist a call.

    "No, Rod." Lachlan murmured next to me. I looked at him to see if he had woken up but he hadn't. He must be dreaming. But Rod? I thought about it and figured it must be dreaming about his brother Roderick. He had been killed back when we were around eighteen. The family took it really hard, but thinking back on it. Lachlan never was the same after that.

"Please." He begged. Something in his voice made my heart hurt for him. Something wasn't right.

"Lach. Baby, wake up." I spoke softly, hoping not to startle him too much. Quicker than I thought humanly possible, Lachlan was up and out of bed. Holding a gun towards my head. HOLY FUCK.

"Lachlan. Put the gun down." I may have seemed calm on the outside but I was freaking out a little on the inside. I'd never seen a gun in real life. Where did he get it? Was it tucked into his boxers the whole time?

He stood there staring at me like I was an enemy. His chest was moving in short, sharp breaths.

"Lach." I tried again, this time his eyes widened, and he lightly dropped the gun.

"Fuck!" He bellowed and gripped at his bed ridden hair. I sat there in the bed, not knowing how to react.

"Dammit Lily, I can't do this." He sat on the bed and put his head in his hands. His posture was one of defeat. That I couldn't allow, I needed him to fight. Crawling over to his side of the bed I wrapped my body around his back.

"It's ok. I'm here. We're here." I whispered into his skin. His body was tense, and barely containing whatever was going on in his head.

After a few minutes of stillness, he pulled away only to get back in bed with arms open.

"Can I hold you?" His voice was so different than the alpha Lachlan I was beginning to know. Right now he was vulnerable and needed me. I crawled in immediately and kissed his chest.

"Do you need to talk about it?" Unsure whether or not I should probe or not my hands lightly rubbed him in comfort.

"Just remembering when Roderick died." I was right about him dreaming about his brother. He took a few deep breaths and I kissed him again on the shoulder.

"He was murdered right? We moved to the states right after. I'm sorry, Lach." I lifted up to look into his eyes. He held so much pain on his shoulders. I wished he would lay some on top of mine. Together, we could climb out of the darkness that laid claim to his soul.

"Yeah." He didn't elaborate and I could tell he didn't want to talk more about it. Instead, I laid my head back down and changed the subject. I racked my brain for something to get his mind off of his brother's death.

"Remember when we broke into Tasy's old store and ate every piece of bubble gum in that big bucket. I swear I don't know which was more sore. My cheeks from chewing or my ass from mama beating my hide." I smiled remembering our fun times back in the day.

"You were a little hellion." I could feel him smile in my hair.

"What about the time we saran wrapped Christy's car when she started that rumor about me being an alien in high school." I can honestly say I did not regret that one bit. Christy was a total bitch. I don't really know what she had against me. I wasn't cool or anything, so no clue why the most popular girl would feel threatened by me.

"She wanted me back then. Thought you were competition for my affections." It was like he knew what I was thinking. His voice was starting to turn back to the Lachlan I was getting to know.

"Well, Christy Barns can suck it now." I hoped I ran into her one day with Lachlan's arm around me. I'd play that shit up. Lach's body started shaking beneath me. He was laughing. His chuckle was something that should be bottled up and sold to the lonely women all over the world. It could make any heart swoon and fill with happiness.

"Christy Barns can suck it now." He repeated. I soared on cloud nine with the feelings of making him forget about his nightmare. I could do this. We could do this. After his laughter died down, we fell into a silent walk down memory lane. I wanted to hear everything from his point of view and compare it to my own of events. I was starting to think maybe he had gone back to sleep until his hand roamed down and lightly touched my breast. I bit my lip to stop myself from making any noise. His body slowly moved so we were facing each other. When his lips found mine there was no holding back the sigh of contentment that fled me. Our legs and arms tangled, trying to get closer to one another.

This time there was no rush, we weren't on an open stage. We could take our time, explore each other's bodies. Blood running hot, breaths gaining speed, every part of me wanted to connect with his.

Chapter Sixteen
Lily

Then his phone rang.

"Shit." He cursed and rolled over to grab his phone.

"Yeah." He answered, sounding pretty pissed at whoever dared interrupted us. I couldn't blame him, I was tempted to tell him to take that gun of his and shoot them in the foot. I was very much wanting what was about to happen.

"Right, I'll be there." My heart sank, he was leaving. Now? He turned towards me and groaned.

"Ma needs me to take Aiden to school." As much as I needed an orgasm right now, the need to laugh at his pain bubbled over. I couldn't help it at all.

"You're so going to get it later." He leaned in to kiss me then rose off the bed to get dressed. His cock was hard and looked to be making getting his jeans up a difficult task. Poor guy.

"I'll pick you up from self-defense later, ok? We can go have dinner somewhere." He rolled his shirt over his head. Dinner with Lachlan sounded great to me!

"OK, we'll be at Rangers tactical. I think we get done around 3." I was getting excited about my day of kicking ass, stuffing my face, and sexing Lachlan. I had much to look forward too. He nodded, taking in the information I'd relayed and grabbed his gun, tucking it into the back of his pants. I made a mental note to ask him about that later. I needed to know if I would be feeling and seeing guns all over the place.

"Gotta run." He leaned down to kiss me one more time before heading out the door. My body fell back on the soft bed with a smile. Lachlan, the dangerous man, was out taking his little brother to high school. It was comical but showed exactly what I'd always known. He was not a bad man. No evil would ever go out of his way, leaving a willing woman behind to help family.

I looked over at the clock to see it was only six in the morning. I had a lot of time to waste before class and seeing Lach again. Feeling energized I hopped out of bed and went straight to the bathroom. I needed to pee and take a nice long shower.

After feeling refreshed, I got dressed, and made a fruit smoothie to keep the day rolling, which actually went by pretty damn fast. I went to yoga class, and the school to do some routines that had been flooding my brain. After cleaning up and getting into another set of work out clothing, Nera picked me up at the house and together we went to our class.

"I'm excited." I beamed as we stretched on the soft mats. The teacher was a retired green beret, and had experience with how self-defense saved his daughter's life. So he wanted to make sure everyone knew the basics.

"So you and Lachlan are doing great now?" Nera asked while she reached down to touch her toes. I was in the mood to girl gab so I was happy she initiated it first.

"I think we are, although he had some nightmares last night that could have been bad, but we made it through." We were going to be ok. Nera came up and widened her legs to get a deeper stretch. She was almost as flexible as me. Impressive.

"I can imagine, shit he's seen." She comments so matter of fact like. It made me curious, and even though I know the saying about the the curious cat, I couldn't help myself.

"Like what happened with you?" I prodded. I knew a little bit about the whole thing.

"Yeah, that was intense. But my therapist thinks I am really coming through the whole ordeal. Thank God for Lachlan, like you, if he hadn't of saved me, my life would be way different." She walked over to take a sip of her water. Lachlan saved her? That was something new. I wanted to ask her to explain more but the instructor started the lesson.

We went through the basics of stopping an attacker with a knife, gun, and unarmed. It was interesting to learn that no matter what way they came at you there was a counter attack to get out and get away. But not even kicking a guy in the nuts soothed the growing question in my head about Lachlan. I needed to know more. When the class was over Nera and I both agreed that we wanted to take another. We wanted to be completely proficient at getting away from any potential threat. I looked out of the glass doors to the studio and didn't see Lachlan's SUV anywhere so I voiced my thoughts to Nera.

"I know you don't know me that well, but I'm dying over here. When you said he saved you, what did you mean?" She looked at me in confusion and spoke.

"Like how he got you out of that shit hole? He got me out of my stepparent's house." I was completely shocked by her statement. I had no clue.

"I figured since you two were together that you knew what he does?" She was trying to get a read on me now, well good luck. I had no clue how I was feeling right now. I shook my head no.

"I owe him my life. And whether he likes what I'm about to do or not. I believe you two were made for each other, and if you're as serious as you sound about him I will tell you some information."

"I can't have you do that. He could get super pissed at you!" I didn't want to cause conflict between them. They had something that most people longed for, a special kind of friendship. She wrapped her hand around my wrist and pulled me off to the side, out of the way of anyone who could hear us.

"Let me worry about that. Do you love him?" She was giving me the look that said she meant business. I nodded.

"I always have." It was true, and even though I knew I wasn't going to like what she said, I would still love him afterwards.

"Lachlan is a hired hand. Wolfe had him go in and get me out of my personal hell. He brought me justice and salvation. He is deadly, and fierce, but is the best man I know. If anyone can deal with the things he does. I believe you can."

"Enough!" Lachlan's hushed tone from behind us scared us to hell. Busted.

"Get in the car, Lily." He barked at me. I looked at his face, he was pissed. But he wasn't pissed at me. He was pissed at Nera. I did as he said but as soon as he got in the car it would be on.

"You deserve more Lachlan. She is your more." I heard Nera say to him as I walked out the door and got inside the black SUV that was waiting for me. Nera walked off to her car like she didn't just tell secrets about a mercenary. She was sticking by what she said, and not even Lachlan's evil glares could scare her.

I watched as he stood there for a minute before getting in the car. He was silent and his movements were forceful as he started the car and took off.

"I'm not afraid." It was the truth. Even though I was probably not fully computing what Nera said about him, I wasn't afraid of him.

"You should be. Fuck, did you even hear what she said?" His hands were white knuckling the steering wheel.

"Yeah, she said you were a hired hand and that you saved her." He started laughing. It was a strange reaction to what I admitted. He turned off the busy street and took us away from Portree, out to the country.

"Did she mention how I cut off a few of her step cousin's fingers?" The blood drained from my body. He did what?

"Yeah, soak that up. I also beat the shit out him and both of her stepparents. For every time that fucker touched her while she laid there, numb to the world. For every time she stood up to them and they spat in her face."

I didn't even know what to think.

"Those shit stains who took you? Yeah, they all paid for that too. Still want to love a killer, Lily?" He was angry, but at who I wasn't so sure anymore. I didn't say anything, because right now I didn't know what would come out of my mouth. I honestly didn't know.

"Shit." He cursed.

"What?" Alarms were going off in my head. He looked in the review mirror and back to the road.

"Tighten your seat belt, and hold on. We're being followed." He put his foot to the pedal and faster on the open road we went. I looked behind us just as something broke the back window.

"Oh my God!" I screamed and ducked down.

"Stay down!" Lachlan called out to me. I was scared, holy hell was I scared. A gun fired and hit the SUV a couple more times, hitting the windshield, and the back seat. Whoever the shooters were thankfully sucked at the moment. Lachlan swerved the car back and forth as we were continuously being shot at.
"Shit. Lily. Sorr..." Before he could finish saying sorry something exploded right to the right of us and the car took to the sky. I know we flipped and crashed landing upside down, but other than that I didn't know shit. Was I even still alive? Does your body still hurt when you're dead? I wouldn't think so, things were supposed to be nice and peaceful.

"Lily!" Lachlan shouted. I felt him hold me tight while undoing my seat beat. Nope not dead yet. Slowly my eyes opened to see his face marred by little cuts and blood. I'm sure I probably looked like that or more.

"This is gonna hurt." He warned as he did his best to get me out of the wreckage. I wanted to help him, but right now I felt like a limp noodle and was afraid to move anything out of fear of injuring it more.

    I heard some people yelling and car doors slamming. Then I remembered the reason we were in an accident in the first place, we were being shot at. I looked at Lachlan with wide eyes. We were about to die.

Chapter Seventeen
Lachlan

I was going to tear those fucker's limbs from their torsos for putting that looking on my starlight's face. Not only did they shoot at her, but they used a rocket launcher to blow her up.

"Stay low, I'll be right back. I promise." I kissed her cut up forehead and went back to the squished SUV. I reached in and grabbed my berretta, an extra clip, and my leg holster of knives out of the glove box. I watched through the windows of the car as four sets of legs were walking our way. Dead men walking.

They split up, two by two walking around the sides of the SUV. I looked back and didn't see Lily, but knew she was in the ditch I laid her in. I hoped she stayed there and didn't watch this. But maybe if she did she would see the killer I was, because I'll be damn if I was going to let these men live.

The crunch of broken glass beneath their boots was a dead giveaway to their location. These men were obviously amateurs. Moving with absolute silence of a well-practiced hunter, I snuck to the left and saw the shadow of the two men. The men on the other side were opening doors and checking inside the wreck. With my gun in my right hand, I reached down with my left and grabbed a knife. These were stealthy, and slick.

    I focused on the men in front of me and when the first man took a step and came into view I knocked him to the ground with a sweep of my leg and threw the knife upwards towards the man behind him. Hitting him right in the throat. He gurgled on the blood that was pouring out before he fell to the ground. The first man was grabbing his gun that had twisted around his back in the fall and started yelling for the others. I looked at them as they came around and started shooting. Rolling over as he struggled, I grabbed his bullet proof vest and hoisted his upper body up as a human shield. They shot into him trying to get to me. I felt a shot hit my arm but I paid no mind to it. It was only a flesh wound. Tossing the dead shield to the side, I rolled to the side of the car giving me more stable cover. I heard the crunch of glass again but it seemed more hesitant. They should have looked up who they were trying to kill before they came at me. I was no thug with a gun.

    Then I heard it, that little gasp. No.

I looked over to see Lily up and peeking at the scene. The two gunmen turned towards her and started shooting. Fuck no! I stood and aimed. Firing only two bullets, one to each head. Kill shot.

"Lily!" I shouted at her as my feet took off. She was curled up into fetal position but otherwise ok. Her head popped out of her position to see if everything was ok.

"It's over, come here." Anything I was feeling earlier in the car was gone. I just wanted her to be ok. I didn't care if she said she never wanted to see me again, as long as she was safe and not hurt. I'd live.

I fell to my knees right beside her and she crawled up onto me. My arms latched onto her like a leech. I never wanted anything like this to happen. She stayed silent but I could feel tears staining my shirt. My heart twisted.

"Come on, let's get you to the hospital." I scooped her up, and not even my bullet wound was going to stop me from carrying her to the gunman's car.

"But what about them." She looked at the bodies on the ground. Such ugliness.

"Please don't look at them." I begged. I didn't want her to see what I did. She didn't say anything or even nod, but she did look up at me, wanting something. I gave her the only thing that came to mind about her question.

"We leave them. Someone will be down this road eventually and they will call the police. An investigation will happen but they won't find anything." I opened the door to their 4x4 truck, and made sure she was settled before going back to the wreck. I reached down in through the back glass hatch and grabbed two items.

Gasoline and a lighter. After dousing everything, grabbing my knife from the man's throat, I tore off a piece of my shirt and lit it, tossing the material into the wreck. The flames engulfed the whole scene as I walked away. I hoped maybe to Lily it looked like an action movie where the hero was walking away with fire behind him instead of the dangerous killer hiding the evidence of his work.

When I opened the door to the truck I saw her flinch a little, making me hate myself even more. I started the truck and headed towards the hospital.

"So that's what you do?" Her voice was small. I took a deep breath and answered. If I was already burning in hell for my actions at least I should be honest about. No use hiding things with her any more. She saw it first- hand. Even Nera had seen my handy work but didn't see me actually do it. She was the one to pull the trigger on them.

"Yeah. I get jobs, do the work no one wants to be tethered to. Usually for the government or the wealthy."

"How did you know to save me?" That heart of mine that was already twisted, started to crack.

"I wasn't there for you. I was hired to get three girls that were taken, out. Thank all the stars in the sky that I happened to step into your cubicle and see you. Worst fucking moment of my life." The memory of her lying in that bed with IV's stuck in her arms would forever haunt me. I was reliving that moment in my head when a soft touch on my arm startled me. I looked over at her with wide eyes. How could she stand to touch me right now? Why was her gaze beaming with love?

"Thank you." I scoffed, she wouldn't be thanking be in a minute.

"Don't Lily. God can't you see how fucked I am. I just killed four men!" I needed to get through to her!

"They were going to kill us." She countered, while true, killing was killing and every time you took a life the action took a piece of your soul. I always wondering when it was going to be too much.

"I killed all those men that took part in taking you. Blew their whole operation up." I was actually proud of that day.

"Saving probably hundreds of other women from a terrible fate. Lachlan. I get it. I really do, and while I may not like it one hundred percent. All you've proven to me is that you only kill bad people. People who, I'm sure I'll go to hell for saying this, but are better off not on this earth anyways." Those words coming out of my sweet Lily's mouth sounded dirty and terrible. I wanted to wash her from head to toe and clean her lips with soap. I groaned but didn't say anything.

"Have you killed any children?" My face scrunched up in disgust.

"No. It's in all my contracts, no children." I could see where she was trying to go with this but I did the only thing I could think of. I needed to out the worst sin of all. She wouldn't be able to look at me after what I was about to tell her, but I truly felt it was the only thing left to say.

"I killed Roderick." I admitted. Her gasp was so quiet but it felt like it shook my whole body.

"Lach." She covered her mouth with her fingers.

"He'd gotten in trouble with some bad guys. Being only a few years older than me at eighteen I thought we were pretty cool friends. Then he started keeping things from me and I got pissed. He took mom's car one night and I followed him, determined to figure out what he was hiding. I watched him walk into a shady looking warehouse with a few other men and went in to keep watching.

I watched them beat him, and tie him to a chair. My older brother. I came out from my hiding spot and punched some of the guys trying to get him free. I tried. God, Lily, did I try." The whole scene flashed through my mind like it was right before me.

Roderick had blood in his brown hair, and his green eyes were starting to swell. But he pleaded with me to leave, telling me he was so sorry and he loved me, and our other brothers.

"What happened?" Lily's voice brought me back to the present and I continued on.

"The leader of the gang told me all about how my brother was involved. He wasn't anything bad, but he was their errand boy and he wanted out. The only way to leave was in a box."

I hate that saying. "The leader being the lowest of the low made me a deal. He gave me a gun and told me to shoot him. If I did, my brother would go free. If I didn't, Roderick would die." I gripped the steering wheel to help ease the pain in my chest but it did nothing. I heard the gun shots in my head, and the pain in my chest throbbed. The light leaving my brother's eyes haunts me every night.

"You couldn't shoot the leader." Lily figured it out.

"Nope, I was too chicken shit to shoot him and save Roderick. So he shot him right there. He died with my name on his lips. Of course, seeing that gave me the rage I needed to pull the trigger on the leader." My first kill. And I was so leveled by seeing my older brother die that in my rage I also shot the man who pulled the trigger. His buddies ran from the warehouse and I fell to my knees in a puddle of my tears and blood. Blood from the enemy and blood of family.

"I'm so sorry." I could hear her tears through her voice. It was pure ugliness in its raw form. That moment was the exact moment I knew my life would never be the same. I would never have the girl I'd loved, I could never be home with my parent's for random dinners, or have a future of light and happiness. Nope, I demolished that dream with the wrecking ball of a pulled trigger.

Chapter Eighteen
Lachlan

    We drove the rest of the way to the hospital in silence. It was a lot to take in, and I really hoped it was settling in with her. When we pulled up to the emergency room, I got her out and vowed that after she was checked out and everything was fine I would disappear again. I wanted things to work, but it hadn't even been 24 hours and she was getting shot at and things were falling apart. I'd even fought it a couple times in that 24 hours.

    Nurses rushed towards us and got us into a room. I told them I was not going to be separated from her, even if right now she wanted to be as far away from me as possible. I sat on a chair while nurses cleaned her wounds on the table, and tried to touch mine.

    "Sir, please I need to look at your arm." I looked up at the redheaded nurse who was staring at me expectantly. She reminded me so much of Ma that I simply nodded and let her work on my arm. There were nurses in an out of the room for about an hour before we were cleaned up as best as we could be. Lily was taken back for X-rays and now we were waiting for the doctor to come in and discuss if anything was injured beyond what we could see.

"Don't leave me." Lily looked at me and whispered. I wasn't going to leave her right now. Not until she was safe back at her apartment. After waiting maybe another ten minutes, the curtain opened and a tall man most likely in his upper thirties walked in and he looked familiar somehow.

"Lily Singer. I couldn't believe my eyes when I saw your name on my chart." This doctor knew Lily. I watched her face as her body froze and her eyes darted to the doctor. She had a look of utter surprise, and not exactly excited to see this man.

"Jarred. What are you?" She couldn't even finish her question. I looked him over, searching for signs that he was a threat to her. He was about average weight, nothing was overly toned but he didn't have a beer belly. He had blonde hair and was clean shaven. He was dressed for the part of a doctor. I got a strange feeling from him, but not one of a killer. This man had never handled a gun before. Still something was off.

"I travel for work. You remember that. Lance and I have a cousin in Portree, and when I can visit, I try to get a job close to family. I'm also subbing at the local community college for a few weeks while I'm here." That's where I recognized him from. He was the man that was getting into his car in the parking lot yesterday as Lily and I were leaving the school. So far everything was adding up, but it still didn't explain how they knew each other.

"Jarred is my ex-boyfriend's brother." Lily answered my unspoken question. I took in the information but gave no indication that it pleased me or upset me to hear her statement.

"Yeah, he told the family about that. We're sorry it didn't work out. We thought you guys were really good together." He spoke and I saw him glance my way once. If he wasn't here to look over Lily, I might have punched him for saying that in front of me.

"So, am I free to go?" Lily piped up to break the tension. I was eager to hear what the results were.

"Well, you have a concussion, and a sprained right shoulder but other than that you are very lucky. I've seen cases like yours in bad car accidents that ended up a very different way."

Terrible bedside manner. Really? This was a doctor teaching young minds.

"So I can go?" She tried again. Anxious to leave.

"Yes, just let me check a few cuts on your head and I can sign off on your discharge papers. But you need someone to stay with you over night and wake you up every two hours. Ice, and rest will be your best friend for the next couple days." He set the chart down and put on some latex gloves. When his fingers touched her hair, I saw her flinch slightly. It must have been painful.

"Ok, all good." He took a step back and smiled while removing his gloves.

"I'll get everything ready for you to sign and you can go." He looked at her and didn't acknowledge me. Prick.

"Thanks." She murmured.

"If you need anything at all, or feel dizzy please give me a call. Here's my cell." He handed her a card from his pocket. I saw his pointer finger sneak out and touch her intentionally. I growled at his intent to caress her. He looked at me and I saw nothing. No remorse or fear. He didn't care at all that I could beat his ass. I laughed on the inside. He was like the men that hired me. Money could buy anything, including men like me. He would probably think he could take me out with dollar signs or hire a bigger, badder guy to take me out. Never.

"Have a goodnight." He walked out of the room and I notice Lily let out a deep breath in his wake.

"I don't like him." I told her, she looked at me and nodded.

"I never really liked him either. He always reminded me of the type of guy that would sniff dirty panties." Interesting way to put it but maybe that was the vibe I was getting from him. A few minutes later a nurse came in and had us sign some paperwork. When we were free to go, I helped her into a wheel chair and the valet brought the 4x4 out for us. She went into my arms willingly so I could get her into the truck and buckled.

We rode back to her apartment in silence. I didn't know what to say and I had a feeling she was done with me. After everything that was now out in the open, she would realize the depth of my darkness.

When we parked in front of her bright building, I turned off the car and looked at her.

"That's why you left that night wasn't it? It makes so much sense now." She sounded like she finally figured out the puzzle of life.

"Yeah." I knew what she was talking about. The night I left her, she kissed me. I had just killed a man the night before and couldn't handle it. She was too pure for me then and she was still too pure for me now. I don't even remember much of that night besides she said she wanted to try something and then she kissed me. I gave in for two seconds but then stopped and made up an excuse to leave. And then I didn't see her for two years until that night I watched her perform. After that night I stayed away for another six years, until she showed up in my life in the worst way imaginable.

"I don't hate you, Lachlan." Her words were sweet and soothed a part of me. She didn't hate me. Even after everything she didn't hate me, but she wasn't saying anything else. It squashed a little ray of hope that was crawling up from my depths

"Let's get you in the apartment." I wanted to get her inside, where she could rest. I got out of the truck and walked to her side. Carefully I eased her out of the truck and she helped me get the door open into her living room.

"I'll stay tonight to watch over you, but tomorrow, Lily, I'm going back to the way things were." I set her down on the couch and told her the truth.

"What are you saying?" She was looking at me with furrowed eyebrows and a very confused expression.

"You know everything about me now. It's too much of a burden to take on. I'm going to do us both a favor and leave. You can forget about the terrible things I've done and move on." I sat on the recliner and settled back. My eyes closed briefly before something hit my face forcefully.

Chapter Nineteen
Lachlan

I sat up and looked at the pillow on the ground.

"Did you just throw a pillow at me?" I was astounded.

"Yeah, you're a dumbass." She grabbed another and chucked it at me.

"STOP MAKING DECISIONS FOR ME!" She yelled. She threw another, I knocked it out of the way and stared at her to knock it off.

"Dammit Lachlan, cut it out. I don't care ok! I love you, I still love you, the good, the bad, the ugly. I want to be there for you, Lachlan. I want to be your home. A place where you can come to and unload some of the boulders on your back. I want to be the salve to your soul. Do I like it that you have killed people? Not really. But you are not a cold-blooded killer. You're a killer with a purpose. You've probably saved more people from heartbreak and living terrible lives than you have from taking a life." She wasn't done.

"And you didn't kill your brother. Don't roll your eyes at me! I know you feel you did, but Lachlan you were eighteen years old. Probably never held a gun in your life. You're not evil. What happened was horrible, and what you did was out of pure emotional rage. Don't run Lachlan. Don't leave. We can do this together. We can be each other's home." She pleaded with me, I shook my head no but even as I fought it in my head, I wanted to give in.

"I'll spend the rest of my life trying to prove to you that you are a good man, Lachlan. Please, give me that chance." She pleaded some more, and my resolve to leave broke. She knew everything. She knew all of my flaws, and skeletons that were hidden in the back of my closet and yet, she wanted me still. We were imperfectly perfect. Right then I believed her. Not about her proving I was a good man, but that together we could be each other's home.

"I love you." I told her before my feet were moving and I crushed my cut lips to hers.

"Always have." I finished during our next breath.

"Always will." She added. I smiled against her lips. That I would.

We kissed as best we could until the tinge of blood touched our tongues. We were in no shape to be doing anything sexual tonight. So instead I carried her into the bathroom and together we washed away everything we could from our afternoon. After we were dry, we laid on the bed, completely naked. There was nothing hidden between us anymore. We worshipped each other's bodies with our eyes, and hands roaming over every curve, every edge. But kept it as simple exploration. We needed to heal tonight, but tomorrow it was on.

"So where do you go in between jobs?" She was curious and I had to admit it was nice not to have to beat around the bush when she asked me questions about my life.

"I have a flat in London and in North Carolina in the states. I'm rarely at either." My hand coasted over the little flare of her hips. She was so soft.

"I have an apartment in New York but I'm not sure if I'm going to go back to it. Maybe I'll rent it out or something." I didn't know what to say to her statement so I just kept feeling her velvety skin.

"Can we be together? When you aren't working?" She nibbled on her bottom lip, showing she was nervous. If she was asking for us to live together that answer was simple.

"Of course, Lily." My finger moved down her stomach and circled her navel.
"Where are we going to stay? My place? Yours?" She wanted to talk out everything right now? I leaned in and pressed a kiss to her lips to shut her up a bit.

"Lily, wherever you go. I'll follow." It was as simple as that. She was my home now, and I wasn't going to give her up for anything. She smiled at my answer and we just laid there in silence until she fell asleep. Once I knew she was out and I wouldn't bother her, I kissed her forehead and covered her up in the blankets.

As much as I wanted to stay in that bed with her, I needed to find out why those men were that came after us today. Wishing I had brought more clothes over to her house, I put on my blood splattered jeans and shirt. After swiping her key and locking the door behind me, I went out to the truck and drove to my parent's house to grab some clothes, and my gear. I needed to scope out everything I could about the attackers. No one heard me at the house because I didn't want them to, so I was in and out in no time. Once I was back at the apartment, I got to work on figuring out every detail I could on those men. In the car was two rounds left of the rocket launcher in the back seat. Just sitting there. I rolled my eyes at the pure amateurisms of their actions. These men were not professional hit men. I looked up the information on the car and the serial number to the guns and found they led back to that shit hole where I'd found Lily.

It would seem there were a few survivors, and they wanted a piece of the man who brought down their operation. One of the men had left his cellphone in the truck, and I'd hacked into all of his information. They found me through finding Lily and were planning on taking her as a hostage if they didn't kill me right away. Out for revenge. Pitiful job they did. They didn't do their research, not that they would find much anyways. Lachlan Sloan didn't truly exist.

After about an hour of digging through the truck, I came to the conclusion that these boys were it. The last of the rebels in that gang who were out to get me. It was one less thing to worry about but I knew there would be more. There were always pissed off bad guys that I'd taken down. It was never completely over, but at least for tonight I could go back to that warm bed with Lily and pull her into my arms and rest. Tomorrow would be another day, but for tonight. I'd enjoy my life.

I'd woken up to the smell of coffee and sugar. Lily wasn't next to me but I heard a few scraping noises coming from the kitchen. I rolled out of bed and went to the bathroom to wash up a little before seeing her. I looked at my reflection in the mirror and saw the bruising and little cuts from the wreck. I looked like I had gotten in a tussle at the bar. Maybe that would be what we told everyone, but then that wouldn't explain Lily's cuts.

I guess as close to the truth was better. We were in an accident, but we're ok. I was wearing long plaid pants and nothing else after changing last night. I was deciding on whether or not to put on a shirt, but chose the latter when I thought about her face when I walked out there wearing nothing but pants. I knew I looked good. Cuts and all, and it was nice to see the blush on Lily's cheeks when her body agreed with that statement.

Chapter Twenty
Lachlan

"Smells good." I walked out towards the kitchen to see her in a cropped shirt and little shorts with socks that came to her knees. Adorably sexy. She peeked at me and I saw that blush I was looking for. She was pure heaven. I wrapped my arms around her from behind and placed my chin on her head. My short, but beautiful girl.

"I made blueberry pancakes. Hope that's ok." She flipped the gooey cake and we watched as it cooked.

"Sounds great. Need any help?" I pulled back to kiss her head and then moved down to her neck. She was soft, and yet hard. I felt my cock responding to her nearness before she spoke.

"Mm. You can, uh...Set the table." My cock was distracting her, that pleased me greatly. She was so responsive to me. Pancakes were forgotten. I reached over and turned off the stove before lifting her up over my shoulder.

"Lach! What are you!" I cut off her scream with a smack to her ass. It was right there next to my face, I wanted to bite it. Kiss it. Worship her perfect ass.

"I'm setting the table." I gently lifted her off of me and laid her across the top. I looked her over like the breakfast she was.

"Delicious." I licked my lips and brought my hands to her legs. Slowly moving up and down her thighs, warming her flesh. She wiggled and I could tell she was just as affected as I was. Gently, I pulled down her shorts to find her commando. I liked that, I liked that a lot. I hummed in delight.

"Breakfast of Champions." I purred. Best breakfast buffet a man could ask for. Unlike our first time on the stage, I was going to savor this moment. There would be no rushed movements. I'd been waiting for so long to truly have her in my life. As mine. I would make this morning last forever if I could.

I started at her toes. Kissing each one before moving towards her toned calves. I could see her sex glisten with desire. It only made me want to draw this out as long as I could. Take everything she had to give and more. I pulled her body slightly so her ass was on the edge of the table. I pulled out her chair and sat down. She looked at me like I was a hot mess. But I also saw in her eyes the anticipation of what was to come. She was enjoying this as much as I was. With a smirk on my lips, I pressed a kiss to her clit. Giving it a little love bite. Her yelp and bowed back made me growl in delight. Her head fell back as I flicked my tongue out and tasted her sweet nectar. She was soaked and I wanted to lick and suck it all from her. Deciding I'd had enough of sweet tastes I went in for the main meal. Devouring her, pressing my tongue in and out of her pussy. Focusing on her clit then back to her entrance. She moaned and wiggled as I took it all.

I felt her start to tense and I eased off. Her frustrated groan made me chuckle.

"In time my little starlight." I kissed her gently under her shirt and the little bottom swell of her breast before coming back from her shirt and helping her peel out of it.

"Why do you call me Starlight?" She moaned as I ran my two fingers around her clit, my other hand pushed down my pajama pants, freeing my cock.

Taking myself in my hands, I ran the head up and down her slit

"Because you are so bright, so pure, and so far beyond my reach." I eased myself into her wet heat. She gasped, her hands clawing at the wood of the table. Slowly pulling out and pushing back into her in the slowest and sweetest way I knew how. Wanting to feel her completely against my body I leaned over and wrapped my arms around her back. Hoisting her up so we were chest to chest. Lips to lips. Her arms wrapped around my neck, holding me to her. I wasn't going anywhere. Every stroke was long, slow, and hard. Our lips connected and each kiss was an unspoken dedication of love. A kiss for every moment missed over the years, and with every kiss she eased a piece of my soul.

 Together we moved until sweat covered our bodies, our breaths were harsh, and the need for release was almost painful. My hands gripped underneath her legs and lifted her up. Holding her impaled on my cock and driven by the desire to satisfy us both, I lifted her up and slammed her back on my cock. Fucking her into oblivion. She fell and screamed into my shoulder moments later. Milking my cock for every last bit of cum I could give. My fingers dug into her skin as my release hit, making me groan into her sweat-matted hair.

 "Not out of reach anymore." She whispered on her breathless lips. I smiled and kissed her. My phone beeped from the bedroom, pulling my mind off my woman. She nipped at my lips.

"Go get that, I'll see if I can salvage any of breakfast for us." She pulled back and I slowly eased out of her. I pulled up my pants and walked to the bathroom to get her a warm wash cloth. She took it and cleaned herself and before skipping off into her kitchen. I shook my head and went in search of my phone. It was a text from Wolfe.

Doing a song at the ArchAngel tonight, you and Lily should come. WOLFE

Going out tonight would be fun. It would be Lily and my official first date out together.

"Hey, Wolfe wants us to go see him sing tonight at a pub, want to go?" I yelled from the bedroom.

"Oh sounds like fun!" She yelled back. I shot him a text saying we'd go.

I didn't have any jobs lined up soon so I could relax with my girl and we could figure our shit out together.

I tossed my phone onto the bed and walked back out to see her setting a plate of pancakes on the table. My memories of that table were forever ingrained in my head. I smiled as I walked over and kissed her on the head before sitting down.

"Sorry there's only a couple." She gave me a knowing look like it was my fault. I smirked at her, I had no regrets about breakfast.

The pancakes were really good, and the rest of our morning was easy. After everything that had went down yesterday, we needed an easy day. We talked about her mom, and I was sad to hear about her passing. She was a fine woman. We had also talked briefly about those men who attacked us. She was worried that more would be coming, so I told her they were it and why they came after us. It seemed to ease the tension in her shoulders a little. I wanted to promise her that shit like that would never happen again, but I couldn't. She understood and was still ok with being with me. It was amazing and I sat there on the couch with her the rest of the day. Holding my woman close while we watching movies, not having any stresses or cares in the world.

Chapter Twenty-One
Lily

    The bar was crowded tonight, and no one even knew that Wolfe was going to play a song tonight. Nera, Lachlan, and I all sat at the bar waiting for him to take the stage.

    I knew I looked like a goof with the big smile that was plastered on my face. Lachlan was mine, and he was done running from me. We were in it together, whenever he felt the world on his shoulders, I would help him carry the weight. And what a weight.

    I shuddered thinking about yesterday's events. Lachlan killing those men without any remorse was something I wasn't sure I would get used to. He didn't even blink as he threw that knife at the man's throat. Granted they were trying to kill us so I really shouldn't be upset, but it was still something I didn't want to see again. Despite knowing, he was a killer, and a good one at that, I still loved him. I believed he only killed evil. It was something I felt my soul was at peace with. He wasn't out slaughtering children; he was taking out the criminals who did pure evil acts in the world.

 His lips touched my head from behind me and I was reminded why I was ok with it all. He was my everything. I needed him in my life.

 The singer on the stage ended his song with a loud strum of his guitar, drawing our eyes to him. After thanking the crowd, he left the stage and Wolfe walked up the stairs and sat on the stool with his acoustic guitar. He hummed into the mic and I saw Nera smile beside me. Instantly I knew what song he was going to sing and I felt chills every time he did it. His fingers started strumming the tune and when he opened his mouth the whole crowd silenced.

You have no peace, can't even sleep
Your demons chase you every day and night
I can't protect you from your dreams
Or promise things will be all right

But darling I
Promise you'll survive
I'll keep your heart alive
And make sure our love will thrive
And darling you

I know you'll see this through
You're beautiful, strong, and true
I'm not one to make promises
But I will for you

    Lachlan's arms wrapped around me, feeling everything while listening to Wolfe sing. It may be his song to Nera, but I think everyone could find a little of themselves in it as well. If I could sing, I'd sing it to my love. I smiled and settled more against Lachlan's chest. Surrounding myself in his warmth and love.

You toss and turn; my stomach churns
At the thought of losing you one more time
Don't ever forget I'm your safety net
When you only see darkness, turn on the light
Darling, I'm your light

But darling I
Promise you'll survive
I'll keep your heart alive
And make sure our love will thrive
And darling you
I know you'll see this through
You're beautiful, strong, and true
I'm not one to make promises

But I will for you

Just carry me with you wherever you go
Only after a storm do you see a rainbow

But darling I
Promise you'll survive
I'll keep your heart alive
And make sure our love will thrive
And darling you
I know you'll see this through
You're beautiful, strong, and true
I'm not one to make promises
But I will for you

When he was done, Nera jumped up from her stool and ran to him. I think that was my favorite part of his shows. No matter how hard she would try not to, she couldn't help herself but to jump into his arms after his beautiful declaration of love to her. The smiles on their faces as they kissed made me laugh, it was nice to be surrounded by love and happiness. I looked back at Lachlan to see him smiling at them too. I leaned up and kissed his chin. When his eyes came down to mine, I saw pure happiness in those green depths. Something I had a feeling that was gone from his life for a long time. I vowed right then that I would forever try to make him happy whenever I could. He deserved it.

"I love you." I mouthed to him. The crowd was going wild at the kissing going on at the stage so I knew he wouldn't have heard me very well. He leaned down and our mouths touched.

"I love you." He whispered against me, his breath tickling my lips. Moving the tiny space between us, our lips joined and mingling in perfect bliss.

"Alright ye love birds, don't want tae give everyone a free show." Wolfe appeared and teased. I bet he was getting a kick out of us. His two best friends were now together.

"Take a piss ye tussa." I gave my shot at a Scottish accent but I was never any good at it. Try as I might.

I pulled away from Lachlan, and looked towards my bearded friend.

"Where's Nera?" I didn't see her attached to him. He nodded towards the restroom. Oh, that was a good idea. I didn't know what else we were going to be doing tonight but I didn't want to be that girl that had to pee as soon as we got there. I jumped off the stool.

"I'm going to go pee!" I blew them a kiss and made my way to the bathroom. Both boys shook their heads but started chatting. It was nice to see them together and happy.

I opened the door and saw Nera washing her hands.

"The boys are so cute together." I commented. She laughed and agreed.

"Yeah, I'd say they have a good bromance going on." I walked into a stall and did my business. After I was done, I walked out and stopped. Nera was standing there looking at the door where two men were pointing guns at us. I didn't know what to think, I was stunned.

Chapter Twenty- two
Lily

"Now, we are going to walk out of the bathroom quietly, if you try to signal your boyfriends we will shoot you. Got it?" The taller of the two spoke. He had a slight Italian accent, with dark brown hair and brown eyes. His shorter companion was blond but very tan with brown eyes. I looked at Nera and she nodded at me. "Ok." We agreed. I tried to think of any way I could signal Lachlan what was happening without them knowing but came up short.

The shorter man walked behind me and put the gun to my back.

"Move." He spat. The tall man was behind Nera as they started moving, I followed behind them. I looked over towards the bar where Lach and Wolfe were but they were distracted by two women. more like trying to fight off two women. I wanted to fight, but that gun was literally touching me and I wasn't that quick.

We made it outside the bar and they led us towards the parking lot where there was a van waiting for us. I heard Nera sigh.

"This again." She breathed. Poor girl, she had complete memory of the last time she was taken. This wasn't my first rodeo either but at least I didn't remember the first time. They opened the door and we climbed in. Once we were all inside and the doors were locked Nera grabbed my hand, holding it tightly. I looked at her, and I felt a bond forming. We were in this together. She wasn't alone this time.

"It's ok." I told her. Maybe because I had just watched Lachlan kill four men yesterday, I was strangely at ease. I knew he would get us, and we would be safe.

"Why did you take us?" Feeling brave I opened my mouth.

"Shut up, you'll find out soon enough. Once we get you to the drop off point, we'll keep your friend for ourselves. Any woman who can keep the interest of a rock star has to have some moves." The blond who was sitting in the passenger seat replied. Yick. I looked at Nera and saw her face turn red. Not in a blushing kind of way but at an almost at her boiling point kind of way.

"Where are you taking me?"
"Someone's paid big money to have you, we're just getting in on the dough."

Someone was paying money for me? Who? What was happening here? The van was silent for another fifteen minutes before the van was slowing down, then finally stopped. They both got out of the van and I whispered to Nera quickly before they opened the door.

"We use what we learned yesterday and run like hell." It was our only choice right now. I wasn't willing to find out who wanted me and I didn't want anything to happen to Nera. She nodded, pissed off enough to give it a go. I wasn't pissed but the need to survive was kicking in through my veins.

When the door opened, I launched myself at whoever was on the outside and took him to the ground. Nera was right behind me as she kicked the other man. I heard his huff behind me but I was focusing on the man beneath me. He had a look of pure shock on his face and I used it. I punched him repeatedly in the nose, he came to his senses and flipped me over. He was much stronger than me. I used my hips and pushed up while bring my hands over my head. He flipped over me and I got in an elbow to the face before getting to me feet.

"Let's go!" I yelled and Nera was right on my tail. I had no clue where we were but we took off. We were in the country outside of Portree. There was small cottage home behind us, I'm guessing that was the drop off point for me. Creepy.

"Let's get off the road." Nera breathed and I agreed. We headed into the woods and kept running. We were both in shape and I knew we could run for a while, but then we were taken to the ground. The men had caught us.

"Get off me!" I screamed and started kicking, punching, anything to get free. I heard Nera struggling next to me, and I was afraid we were losing this battle.

"Get the fuck off my woman." A strong voice bellowed. All heads turned towards the two men standing by us looking fierce with their guns pointed at our attackers. I felt my heart warm at the sight of them. I knew he'd come, and he'd brought Wolfe too. Well, more likely Wolfe wouldn't take no for an answer. I looked at the brown haired man above me.

"You're in trouble now." Yeah, I was rubbing it in but who cares. These assholes were in need of a little ass whooping. His face turned hard like he wanted to hit me but knew his life would be over if he did. I almost wanted him to try.

They got off of us and we both ran towards our men. Nera jumped into Wolfe's arms. His gun dropped briefly while he kissed his woman and whispered against her lips. Once I reached Lachlan, he gave me a once over seeing if I was alright.

"You ok?" he gritted through his teeth. I touched my hand to his face and while he didn't close his eyes in relief, he leaned into my touch. His focus was on the men.

"Wolfe, get the girls back to the truck and take them home." I gripped his shirt after his demand, I didn't want to leave him.

"Go with Wolfe, Starlight. I'll see you soon. I promise." He spared me a glance that made me believe him. I had no clue what he was going to do with those two Italians but I knew it was going to hurt.

Nera held her hand out for me and I clasped it. I gave Lachlan one last look before Wolfe led us to his truck and started taking us home.

Chapter Twenty-Three
Lachlan

Blood had a long time ago become just like water in my mind. I wiped off the blood of the brown headed Italian whose name was Romeo on a dish rag I had grabbed from the kitchen. The cottage they were taking my Lily to was abandoned and the purchaser of Lily was to come and grab her unconscious body at midnight, which was in another hour. Romeo and his companion Trey spilled the beans fairly quickly after a little cutting.

No matter what new ways there were to torture someone, a knife always seemed to work the best. A few slices to the skin between their fingers, then a finger or two. and they were singing like a canary. At first they tried to put up a fight, thinking two against one with a gun would have been easy, until I shot one in the knee and the other in the shoulder. Non-lethal wounds but it would show them I meant business and incapacitate them a little.

Both men were going to bleed out in the next ten minutes after my torture and I couldn't have cared less. They had taken my woman and my Laoch with evil intent. After digging around, I found out they were quite the little criminals. Luring tourists into believing they were fun guys wanting to show girls around beautiful cities after they get off their planes, but then taking them and selling them off to the sex trade. Scum. Using their looks and charms to capture women. Trey told me thinking it would save his life that this purchaser was also the same one who had her taken the first time. He was resilient. Too bad for Trey that his information didn't save his life.

I sat on the couch and listened as their breaths slowed, until they stopped. The purchaser of Lily would be here soon and I intended to find out who the hell was going through such great lengths to have her. I kept my mind off Lily because I knew once I started with those thoughts, I would either have difficulty doing what I would need to do or I wouldn't wait to get information from the man. I would just shoot him as soon as he got out of his car. I was pissed about everything that had happened in the past 24 hours. Just when I was finally seeing happiness with Lily, the brutal reality of my life came crashing in. But this time it seemed like everything had been about her recently. These men weren't after me, and they were unprepared for their target's mercenary boyfriend. Lights coming in through the window brought my attention to back to the mission at hand. Figure out who was behind Lily's kidnappings.

    The car door opened and I peered out from beside the window. It was a man, and he was alone. But before I could get a really good look at him, he jumped back in his car and took off. I took a step back and watched as tail lights sped down the drive and back onto the road. I should have shot his tires, then shot him.

    The Italian's van being parked in front of the house must have spooked him. I looked up towards the heavens and cursed this life. Vowing to all of the universe that I was going to find the mystery purchaser, and do everything in my power to make sure my Lily was safe. I looked at the drained Italians that were sitting at the kitchen table. Knowing that I couldn't leave them here, I dragged them one by one to their van and threw them inside.

Maybe it was the Italian accents but I was suddenly feeling very mafia-ish. I wasn't in the mood to call my contact that cleaned up bodies on my jobs tonight. He was sometimes a surly bastard anyways. Creepy too.

After working some magic and spending about three hundred dollars, the Italians were now swimming with the fishes in the Sound of Raasay, off Portree.

It was about two in the morning when I made it to Lily's apartment, and a light was still shining from inside. I knocked on the door and Lily was opening it and jumping into my arms in the same minute. My arms wrapped around her and I wanted to never let her go. I was home.

"I love you." I whispered in her hair, needing to hear that she still loved me too. God, after everything that had happened I wouldn't blame her if she decided it was too much. Being with a monster.

"I love you so much, Lachlan. I knew you would come for us." She hugged me tighter and I felt my heart soar. I picked her up and she wrapped her legs around me. Clinging to me like a sloth.

"Always, Starlight." That was something she wouldn't have to worry about. No matter what hell we went through, I would always be there for her.

"All good?" Wolfe was sitting on the couch with Nera attached to his side.

"Yeah, you ok little Laoch?" Nera had a very pensive look on her face. She fought with bravery and truly was the warrior I called her. Both girls were. She looked at me and then at Wolfe.

"I want to get married this weekend." That was not what I was expecting to come out of her mouth. Lily turned her body in my arms to look at her with what I'm sure was a confused look on her face. Nera looked around at all of our stunned faces but then stayed glued to Wolfe's.

"I don't want to wait anymore. I want to marry you this weekend." I watched as Wolfe's face lit up the whole room. He was the happiest man alive right now.

"Mah woman wants tae be mah wife this weekend, well looks like we are having a wedding." He kissed her passionately and even though we just went through something awful, maybe this was just what we needed. To celebrate the life and love that we had right now.

"Can we do it at the B&B?" Nera asked between kisses.

"Fuck yes." Wolfe agreed. They pulled away long enough to ask us if we would go and be a part of their wedding. Of course we said yes. I was beyond happy for them and wouldn't miss it for anything. We talked for a half hour about what we needed to do to get the ball rolling and then they left. Off to probably fuck, sleep, and plan.

"Let's go, we need a shower and I need to touch you." I picked Lily up, who had never left my lap to say goodbye and walked us to the bathroom. Slowly, we peeled our clothing off and came back together under the water's spray. When our lips met, and hands started to roam there was no stopping us from taking every drop of pleasure from one another. We tasted, we caressed, we loved.

Once we were dried and in bed, we held onto each other while falling into a deep, peaceful sleep.

The next day was insane. Wolfe wanted to invite my family to their wedding. Ma was going crazy trying to plan how everyone was going to drive the four hours over to Durness where the bed and breakfast was the couple wanted to get married at. It was where their story first started together. It was fitting all around. Mama Lennox was calling Ma constantly chatting about what they could do together to throw this shindig. Honestly, Wolfe and Nera wouldn't have to do anything but show up.

Chapter Twenty- Four
Lachlan

Two days had passed in a blur and we were all driving towards Durness. Ma and Pa were letting Aiden drive the whole way behind Lily and I. Ma was probably having a heart attack while Pa was trying to calm her down so Aiden could focus on driving. In truth, we all knew how to drive very well. Pa would let us drive around the country when we were ten, so we knew our way around a car. Didn't stop Ma from worrying like she always did.

Grant and his family were tailing along too. I'm sure their car was filled with all sorts of annoying noises.

But what was most interesting was Fin. He was coming in tomorrow, because things with the stripper girl were taking a different turn. They weren't together but things we changing. So he was bringing her but she couldn't leave until tomorrow. So all of my family was riding in a long caravan out to meet up with Wolfe and Nera who left yesterday with his mom. I hadn't seen her in so long it would be nice to get together with everyone. And with a happy occasion. Last time I'd seen everyone together was Roderick's funeral. Not great times.

Ma pointed out to me before we left that Roderick's 30th birthday was coming up soon and to remember that they were having a party for him. Lily told her we were still going and I just nodded. Originally I told Ma I would go, but I was planning on leaving and missing it. His death still haunted me, and I wasn't sure seeing his tombstone was something I needed, but still I told Lily I would try. She told me if it was too much that I could go so I would hold her to that.

"I'm so happy for Wolfe and Nera. I mean after Alexis, I didn't know if he would recover." Lily filled the void of silence in the SUV I'd grabbed since I burnt my other ride.

"Yeah, he and Nera are meant to be." I truly believed that.

"You believe in soulmates?" It didn't take me long to think about it.

"Yeah, you?" Not sure why this topic was intriguing but it made me curious if maybe she thought we were soulmates.

"I do. I know we've talked about it before but it really has only been you, Lach. I've dated here and there but you've been the only man that's held my heart. I think like the myths of the land our story was written in the stars, destined to for heartbreak, love, and otherworldly happiness." She smiled and I wanted to kiss her, taste that happiness that was beaming from her lips. There wasn't really much to say after her comment. I just paid attention to the road, while Lily would occasionally ooh, and aah over the beautiful Scottish scenery.

By the time we arrived in Durness, the tiny town was quiet, like everyone was taking a nap. But on the other hand that was Durness. I'd been here once with Wolfe when we were kids but other than that it was his go to place when he needed to escape reality. The water crashing against the cliffs, the little beach areas were you could relax to the smell of the salty sea spray. I could see the appeal. It was peaceful.

"Wow." Lily jumped out of the car as soon as I put it in park. The bed and breakfast was cute, white and wooded. The caretakers Evan and Aggie were talking with Wolfe just outside the house. Evan and Aggie were sort of a short and stocky couple, but the few times I'd met them they had really big hearts. Taking in people and cooking, cleaning, and opening their home to strangers. The Spurtle, which was their pub that Evan ran was not far off beside the B&B, had a few people coming in and out of but being that it was only the afternoon they wouldn't pick up until dinner time.

"There is the crew." Wolfe walked over to us and hugged Lily.

"This place is amazing! I can't believe I've never been here before." She was practically jumping out of her skin to go and look over everything.

"That it is." He set her down and gave me a nod. No need for bro hugs right now.

One by one my family member's came up and said hi to Wolfe and went inside the B&B. Evan was awesome enough to hook us all up with a room for two days.

"Hey guys!" Nera waved as we walked into the kitchen area. She had a biscuit stuffed in her mouth. She did love biscuits.

"Hey, Future Mrs. Lennox." Lily teased and went to hug her. They had truly formed a real friendship in the past few weeks. I was happy for both of them. Nera needed some more friends, and I wasn't sure about Lily's situation but I knew their relationship was perfect all around.

"Gah, I'm not sure I'll be able to get used to that." She rolled her eyes. Such a little shit. She was wearing her signature sweater, and jeans outfit. Lily was rocking her sweater and leggings look. Two peas in a pod.

"So what's on the agenda? Do you need any help?" Lily was a giver. Wanting to help in any way possible for those she cared about. I walked over to the bar stool and took a seat. I needed to hear what all they were going to say, because I would probably be drafted into helping, but I also knew this may take some time.

"Well, we've decided to have fun with our wedding. Ceremony is tomorrow before lunch out by the water. Then we will be throwing a highland game with a big lunch buffet!" Nera was full of happiness right now, something I was beyond elated to see in her.

"That is so cool! Hot guys in kilts, sounds like a good day to me." Lily joked but threw a wink at me. Wolfe was the one to wear a kilt in our little group, I was not. I may be Scottish in my roots but I'd lost that part of me when Roderick died. My job required me to be anonymous. No tattoos, no way to figure out who I was, including a Scottish accent. I knew every once in a while it would slip out, that I couldn't help. But for the most part, one would never know that about me.

"Kilts." Nera mumbled but blush grew on her cheeks. Interesting.

"Awesome, so can we do anything?" Lily volunteered us again.

"I think everything is good for now. Tomorrow I'm sure you can lend a hand somewhere to help get things set up." I'm sure she was right; the night before wasn't really where all of the chaos began. Tomorrow would be a different story though.

"Can I show you some things?" Nera asked Lily, who was nodding so fast I worried she would get whiplash.

"Yeah, of course." Lily walked over to me and kissed me really quick before following Nera up to where they were going to probably talk wedding stuff. Weddings like this didn't take much money, but with Wolfe being a rock god, as Nera called it, he could do whatever he wanted. You wanted something right away, no problem. I stayed on the bar stool and let my mind wander. What type of wedding would Lily want? God, would she even want to get married. I knew I shouldn't have been thinking about this shit right now, considering we technically just got together but It had been a long time coming. I was just fighting to stay away. I could have been with her the whole time.

"No sense in going down that path." I mumbled aloud to myself. Should of, would of, could of. It was pointless to dwell.

I sat there in the kitchen for a few more minutes before going in search of Wolfe, he was sitting on the beach strumming his guitar. Wolfe's music always soothed me, back when we first met, he saved me from drowning. When I was stuck inside from a broken leg, he stayed inside with me, playing his guitar and saving me from being bored. I plopped down beside him and stared out over the Scottish waters. Finding peace in the moment.

"Figure out who took the lassies?" He asked while playing with his strings. I had looked into it. Only people I could come up with was Lance, Lily's ex-boyfriend. The brother who was a doctor, and an unknown we haven't met yet. I didn't have much to go with. The Italians told me that someone wanted Lily really badly, but they didn't have a name.

"Sort of, someone is after Lily. They took Nera because she was there and they wanted a piece." Scum. Wolfe's tune faltered for a moment but he continued playing.

"Ye took care of it?" Anger was laced in his tone. Couldn't blame him, I was still pretty livid that they were taken. Right from under my nose too. Shit like that wouldn't happen again. I was alert now that someone was out there.

"Yeah." I muttered. Wolfe just nodded and looked out over the water. We stayed silent in our thoughts until he asked me something I thought unexpected.

"Wanna be mah best man?" He stopped playing and looked at me. In all the years I'd known Wolfe, he'd never judged me. I was a killer and he'd never cared. He was my brother.

"Yeah." I answered, but then added in one condition.

"No kilt for me though." No chance in hell I'd do that. He laughed and stood up.

"No kilt for ye." He agreed. I got up to my feet and we walked back to the B&B, no telling what the girls were up to. Probably needed to check in on them. They were chatting about nothing special, Aggie called us down for dinner. The lot of us settled around the table, but some even had to sit in the kitchen or in the living room. There was quite a little crowd for the wedding. Ma Lennox showed up late that night after having to go take care of some things but was cracking everyone up at her arrival. Wolfe's ma was pretty much a celtic hippie. She was in her fifties, and had long curly brown hair. She was thin, but tall. She wore a flowing green and blue dress with long sleeves. Her and Ma screamed in excitement at seeing each other. She then moved on to the bride and groom. Hugging them both tightly.

"Oh my, look at this stud. Lach, ye have turned into quite the lad." She whistled and winked at Lily.

"Pleasure as always, Lisa." I kissed her cheek and she slapped my cheek lightly. After she found her place to sit with food, we all ate and talked for hours. When it was finally time to go to bed, Lily wrapped herself around my body and we were surprisingly worn out. Sleep found us quite rapidly, which I was grateful for. I wasn't in the mood to be wide awake with worry about the girl in my arms. The purchaser would show his face soon, and I would make him pay for every ounce of hurt he's caused my little Starlight.

Chapter Twenty- Five
Lily

I knew his family was all around us, but I really couldn't help myself. Lachlan was lying beside me, in just pajama pants. I wanted to taste him, pleasure him. Things have been so hectic between him first arriving and then the wedding that was happening today. He didn't move as I slid down and extra slowly pulled the waistband of his pants down. Not enough that I could release him completely, but enough to get him to rise to me. Looking back up at his beautiful face, which was still asleep, I felt happy.

My life was on the ups and I couldn't wait to see where it took us. My hot breath caressed his cock, making it and the rest of him twitch. His abs flexed and I was drawn to them. His stab wound was pretty much completely healed. But even with all of his little scars here and there, he was still the most gorgeous man I'd ever known.

My fingers lightly touched the velvety skin and moved gently. His cock was stirring to life and I was getting wetter with every inch it grew. I'd had three lovers before Lachlan and they were all boys compared to him. Truthfully, I've always felt like I belonged to him so no one else was compared.

I looked up at his face to see his eyes closed but his eyebrows were pinched. I would fix that look soon. I took him in my mouth and swirled my tongue around. His hips lifted and his hands went to my head. My eyes flicked up to his to see him staring at me. He was awake now, good.

Now I could really play. I increased my suction and bobbed my head up and down. Faster and faster. Then slow it down to almost teasing strokes and licks. His mouth fell open and a soft groan fell from his lips. I loved the sound of him groaning, losing control and just feeling the pleasure I was giving him. It made me feel powerful. His fingers laced through my hair, almost like he was afraid I'd leave his cock. No way. I was right where I wanted to be.

"Lily, I'm gonna come." His hips were lifting in sync with my movements and I was eager to taste him. My hand moved over his balls and I added a swirl of my head and he was coming down my throat. His whole body tensed and his head fell back onto the pillow. His groan, even though was silent so we wouldn't wake anyone, was loud to me. I felt every bit of his pleasure. When he was finished I gave the head of him a quick kiss and sat up.

"Morning." I smiled. Today was going to be an epic day.

"Morning." His voice was all hoarse and sexed out. I liked it.

"We need to have orgasms every day. I like your "I just came" voice." I admitted. I wasn't really one to hold back my thoughts, even when I probably should.

"I like this plan, so now all we need is your orgasm to complete the day." I was going to tell him that I was good for now but he scooped me up and carried me into the pleasant bathroom. Aggie really did a good job decorating this place. It wasn't overboard, but it was nice.

Together we got my shirt and shorts off, and his pants had to go. I turned on the water, that went to hot very quickly and hopped in. Lach looked me over with a predatory glint in his eyes. My pussy was probably dripping from that look, almost like a salivating dog. It knew things were about to get really good.

He lunged at me and lifted me up against the cold tile. I yelped, at first, but then when his lips found mine I couldn't have cared if there was a wall of ice behind me. His cock was pressed against my core. I wrapped my legs around his hips and rubbed myself against him. Needing him desperately.

"Want my cock don't you, Starlight?" He nipped at my neck and flex his hips into me.

"Yes." I moaned. I wanted it very badly.

"You'd let me do anything to you right now wouldn't you?" I nodded, I so would. I was his, forever.

"Marry me, Lily." He whispered into my ear. Before I could even think about what he had just said, he plunged into me and hammered me so hard and so fast against the tile that I was coming in mere minutes. His thrust continued and I held on for my life. My mind was consumed and my body was in euphoria. My legs squeezed around his hips and my nails dug into his back.

"Lily." With a groan he found his release, emptying himself inside me.

When the high of our orgasms started to fall, I was able to think about what he'd said. Did he really mean it? I was scared to say something, what if he said it in the heat of the moment but was having regrets?

"Marry me, Lily." He kissed my cheek and then my lips. Tears sprang from my eyes uncontrollably. He pulled out of me and set me on my feet.

"Shit, Lily. I'm sorry." He cursed and ran his fingers through his hair. Oh no, he thought I was upset.

"Not sorry, Lach. I just…" More tears came and I felt nuts. I wasn't really a crier, but every once in a while something would happen and all the tears that maybe should have fallen at other times would hit me all at the same time. I was beyond emotional and happy. Then I looked through the spray of the shower and my tears to see his face was full of sadness. Oh god, I need to say something.

"Yes!" I choked out and hugged him. His body was completely still, maybe he didn't hear me.

"I want to marry you!" I kissed his chin and started moving up. The violent tears had finally stopped, but he still wasn't moving. Then his arms were crushing around me and his lips crashed against mine then pulled back to speak.

"Fuck Lily, I know we should probably wait but I've fucking waited long enough for you. I want you forever. Mine, my home, my wife. I want to come back to you, and the life we create together. Whatever you want baby, we will have. You want a dog, kids, a fucking home in suburbia, it's yours. You're willing to love me even though you know what I do and who I am, I am willing to give you the world." If my heart could fly out of my chest and into the clouds, it would. That was the most romantic thing I'd ever heard and it had come from the man I loved lips.

"I don't care about any of that, I just want you, you're my home." I smiled and kissed him. A hundred passionate kisses passed between us in that shower before we dried ourselves off and got dressed. I put on a simple long sleeve purple dress that came down to my knees and flats. Nera had asked if I would be her bridesmaid and I told her yes. Thankfully she was easy and didn't care what I wore. Lachlan was dressed in a long sleeve black shirt and dark washed jeans.

"We should probably sit and talk about what we are going to do once we get back to Portree. Do you have any jobs soon?" I asked him and it was strange how the thought of him going off and doing dangerous things didn't really scare me. In my head, he was invincible.

"No, not for another month. What do you want to do when we get back?" He asked while lacing up his boots. I noticed him shoving a shiny little blade into his boot before rolling his jeans over it. I guess that was something I would have to get used to as well. After everything that had happened, maybe it was a good thing he had weapons around him. I sat on the bed and thought about what I wanted.

"Well, to be honest I didn't realize how much I missed Scotland until I got here. I think I'd like to stay for a little while. Maybe I'll see if I could teach some classes at the college or something like that." Teaching could be fun. I loved dancing by myself up on the stage but I also enjoyed helping others with their skill to pursue their passion of dance.

"Ok, we'll stay in Scotland." He shrugged. It was that easy with him.
"Can we get a place?" I bit my lip nervously, we were technically engaged but things were still new.

"Lily, don't be nervous. You want something, I told you, it's yours." He looked at me and I felt more at ease.

"Ok, yeah, I want to get a place together." I told him. He agreed then made me laugh.

"Good idea, I plan to fuck you on every surface I can. Not sure the owners of the apartment would appreciate that. Things could break." He stood and held out his hand for me. I placed mine in his and he hoisted me up.

"Sounds like fun." I smiled and together we walked out of the room and prepared ourselves to be surrounded by happiness and the love for our dearest friends on their wedding day.

As soon as we entered the kitchen, we were bombarded by Wolfe's mom and Aggie.

"Oh thank heavens yer up. Lachlan, Evan needs yer help out in the field. Lily, sweetheart Ah need yer help in here. Then ye need to go see Nera." Aggie handed me two pitchers full of ice water.

"Take those out tae the tables dear." Lisa shoo'd me out the door to the kitchen. Lachlan was right behind me and headed towards Evan, who was setting up a tent in the field next to the B&B. I set the pitchers on the table that was near the tent and got excited. Nera would love this, and by god did she deserve a spectacular day. Knowing that she needed me I went back into the house and to the room she and Wolfe were staying in.

Chapter Twenty- Six
Lily

I knocked and heard Nera yell for me to come in.

"Awesome, thank you for coming. I need your help." I took a step in the door and closed it behind me. Their room was much like ours. One queen size bed, night stand, dresser, and pretty curtains. Simple.

"What's up?" She was in the bathroom when I walked over. She was wearing one of Wolfe's big button up shirts. And only that shirt. I'd been around dancers all of my life. We weren't shy. Having to do costume changes in two minutes would do that to you.

"I'm not a girly type of girl, but I want to look really pretty. I was just never taught how. I figured you could help me." She looked at me with a smile then gestured to a bag of unopened makeup, and as I nodded I felt my heart hurt a little for her. I had a mother, one I loved very, very much. I used to play dress up in with her shoes and makeup all the time. I was a little older than Nera but I wanted to just snatch her up and hold her. Show her all the experiences that she missed. I would be the sister she never had. Teach her all the girl things I knew.

    She sat on the toilet while I added a little bit of blush, hit of purple eye shadow and mascara. Just enough to make her beautiful greyish green eyes pop, then a hint of lip gloss. She was already very beautiful and unique with her Moroccan heritage; she didn't need anything to make her really pretty. She was naturally that.

    "Ok, what should I do with my hair?" She asked and looked over her caramel color hair. All sorts of ideas coming through my head.

    "Well, what does your dress look like?" It really depended on what neckline her dress was. She jumped up and ran into the room, returning with a long white garment bag. We hung it on the hooks behind the door and she slid the zipper down.

    "Wow." The dress was stunning.

    "Yeah, Lisa gave it to me. Saying that even though she never got to wear it, the dress deserved to be part of a special day. It had to be taken in at the boobs because well, she's bustier than I am but otherwise it fit perfectly!" That was actually a sweet story.

"Ok, with that neckline I think we should go with a half up do." I declared and she sat down while I went to work on her hair. I explained things as I went and told her stories about my mom and I playing with our hair and faces. When I was finished, I helped her into the beautiful dress and cute flats. Taking a step back, I looked her over and felt my eyes glisten a little. Today was a day for happy tears I guess.

She stood there and looked into the full length mirror that was by the closet.

"That's me." She looked stunned.

"Yeah babe, you look amazing." She really did. Her hair was wavy, with the front section loosely pulled back and tied low behind her head. We'd put in some embellished pins to add a little sparkle to her hair. But the dress. It was a soft white material. One that had quarter length sleeves, and hugged her torso then flowed straight down to the ground. It was very boho chic. I half expected her to grab a flower crown and put it on her head. But it really worked with her. It had little lace accents that embellished the Celtic culture.

"I'm not sure Wolfe is going to make it through the ceremony seeing you like this." He was going to scoop her up as soon as he saw her and carry her back into the room. She laughed and walked over to the nightstand.

"I guess we'll see. Will you help me put my necklace on?" She handed me the sapphire star necklace Wolfe had gotten her and I clasped it around her neck.

"Perfect." I commented. She was ready and looked amazing.

"OK, you stay here, let me go check on everything and then I'll come grab you. Is someone walking you down the aisle?" We hadn't really talked about the who's and what's of the wedding. She walked over to the window and looked out while staying behind the curtain.

"Yeah, I asked Evan if he would. He said, yes." That was sweet, I told her as much. I opened the door slightly to make sure no one was around before I slipped out to see if everyone was ready.

Everything was pretty much set, considering there wasn't too many people going to the ceremony. I found Wolfe talking to his mom and Lachlan by the beach.

"You guys all set?"

Wolfe was wearing a kilt with his signature tartan colors of grey, black, and red. And a black shirt covering his chest, and boots. He was something else. He didn't go with the full formal Scottish wedding attire, but this was his version.

"Aye!" He confirmed, and Lisa started rounding everyone up towards the little area on the sand where the ceremony would take place. Wolfe took his place next to who I'm guessing was their officiant with Lachlan at his side.

I waved at the window where I saw Nera peeking. I saw a hand with a thumbs up hit the window signaling that she saw me. Moments later she started walking in our direction on the arm of Evan. I walked up to my spot beside the pastor. Even though I kept my eyes on Nera most of her descent, as she got closer and closer, I would peek at Wolfe's expression.

He had a look I would never in my life forget, he was watching the love of his life walk towards him looking like a hippie goddess. She was beautiful, and he knew she was his. After this moment, she would be his in every way there was. My eyes moved towards Lachlan's to see him looking at me. We would have our own special moment soon.

Nera and Evan made it to where we were and he kissed her cheek softly. I could tell my emotions were going to be all over the place today.

When Evan placed Nera's hand in Wolfe's, he pulled her against his body and kissed her senseless. The pastor behind them coughed while holding back his laughter. The couple separated and Wolfe looked at the Pastor.

"Go ahead." He turned back to his almost wife as she blushed brighter than a tomato.

"Welcome friends and family, we are here to celebrate the wedding of Wolfe and Nera."

He continued talking about how life was hard but together they could make it through. They had chosen to do the traditional handfasting ceremony where their hands were wrapped over with a beautiful ribbon. Thus tying them together for all of eternity. Once the pastor declared them husband and wife, Nera leaped into Wolfe's arms and kissed him senseless this time. The small crowd around us cheered and hooted at the couple's display of their love.

Once they broke apart, Wolfe scooped her up into his arms and carried her down the little aisle and over toward the area of the field with the buffet and where the games would take place. A small group of people started to gather around the area and clapped as the couple kissed and waved to the crowd.

I smiled watching them say hello to everyone and thank them for their congratulations all while Wolfe held Nera in his arms. She tried to get out of them a couple of times but then just gave up. Truthfully she was probably lucky he didn't club her and take her up to their room like I thought he would do.

Strong arms wrapped around me and I welcomed them.

"What kind of wedding do you want, Starlight?" Lach's voice was smooth and seductive. I didn't have an answer to that question. As much as I wanted to wear a pretty dress and have a big crowd there to celebrate with, it wouldn't be the same without my mom.

"I don't think I want one." I turned my head and looked into his eyes.

"I just want to be your wife. No theatrics." I didn't know if that was something he'd want. He had a big family and all. Maybe he wanted them to be a part of it.

"You were made for me." He purred before claiming my lips. I was tempted to tell him we should skip the rest of the festivities for the day when his mother came and broke us up.

"Ye can make me grandbabies later. Go have fun with yer friends." She shooed us off towards where the party was getting started. People were making themselves some food, some were dancing to music that had just started playing. Everyone was having a good time and living life the way it was meant to be lived, surrounded by good company and happiness.

    When we made it to the gathering, Lachlan pulled me against his body and we started to sway to the music. We laughed, and danced like we didn't have a care in the world. I should have known things were getting too good to be true.

Chapter Twenty-Seven
Lily

I excused myself to go to the bathroom when a man cornered me. The house was empty at the time and I didn't see him waiting for me in the room.

"I've been waiting for you, Lily. You're hard to get ahold of." He held a gun in his lap, and I just stood there. Not sure what to do.

Recognition of who he was hit me like a wrecking ball.

"John Dowers." I whispered. He was a crazy fan of mine turned stalker until I had gotten a restraining order on him. While I never truly thought he would cause me harm, at the moment I was unsure about that.

"I knew you'd remember me. We always had a special connection." He smiled and I considered that maybe he was just crazy.

"Why are you here?" I stood tall and asked him. His head tilted to the side like he wasn't sure why I was asking him that particular question.

"I'm here for you. I've tried other ways to get you and ran into complications. Figured I'd come and get you myself this time." Oh dear.

"What do you mean you've tried to get me before?" Thoughts were running through my head. Was this the person who was going to buy me from those terrorists? He ran his spare fingers through his brown hair. He was a middle aged man, lost his wife to cancer and fell in love with ballet. I felt sorry for him at first but then he just weirded me out.

"I didn't want to hurt you. I'm sorry I've troubled you. I'm a really good man. I promise. We can go to ballets together; I can take you to nice restaurants." He got to his knees in desperation. I was at a loss of what to do in this situation. I prayed silently that Lachlan was on his way and would stop this before something happened that would ruin the wedding. As if he was answering my prayers, he opened the door with his gun drawn, ready to shoot at any second.

"Who the fuck are you?" Lachlan growled ferociously.

John held tight to his gun but didn't point it at anyone. He was troubled.

"I'm Lily's biggest fan. We are going to be together, where I can take care of her and be her companion." He truly believed those words.

"I don't believe this shit." Lachlan shook his head, I wanted to groan that this was the story of my life apparently but things were still running hot in our room.

"Let's go, Lily. I know I've done bad things, and have hurt you, but I promise we will be good together." He smiled at me and held out his hand for me to take. God, I wanted to help him but I didn't want to go near him. I mean shit, he is the reason I was taken in Milan.

"No John, you need help. We can go talk to someone and get you the help you need. Just give me the gun." I took a step closer and heard Lachlan growl behind me. He did not like that I was walking close to crazy town. But I trusted him. He would shoot John in a heartbeat if he thought I was truly in danger right now.

"No, nothing is wrong with me. You're not her, I know this. I want you. I'm not crazy." Something in him was slipping, and that something was important to his sanity.

"No, you're not crazy. But I feel like you should talk to someone." I spoke honestly.

"No, No! I just need you. If I can't have you then I can't bear the pain." He put the gun to his head. Oh god.

"John, put the gun down." I panicked. This could not be happening. Not right now.

"You have to be with me." He was blackmailing me. Be with him or he would kill himself. My bet is he was nuts enough to do it too. I opened my mouth, still unsure what I was going to say when a loud bang echoed through the room. My eyes closed shut and I was afraid that I would see John with a hole in his head. I didn't want to see that. I'd seen enough carnage to last me a lifetime. Those images would be burned into my mind forever.

"It's ok Lily, you're safe. You can open your eyes." Lachlan's voice filled the room, along with male groans. My eyes flew open to see John on the floor, with the gun on the other side of the room. John was writhing and grabbing his leg which was bleeding onto the wooden planks in the floor.

"It's just a flesh wound. He'll heal." Lachlan told me before grabbing my hand and pulling me against his body. I hugged him so tightly I was afraid I'd pop him.

"I need you to go get the head of the police. He's down at the wedding. Try and keep it as hushed as possible. Ask Evan for help if you need it." He kissed my forehead without taking his eyes off John. I nodded against his chest and ran to find help. I was thankful no one had any inkling as to what was going on in the B&B right now. They were all in a blissful state of wedding happiness. I was a little envious. I found the policeman and asked him to come with me and that we had an emergency. He understood the need for silence but I noticed him unbuckling the clasp that held his gun in place. Calmly, I led him back to where Lachlan and John were waiting in our room. Hopefully not bleeding out to death. When I opened the door, Lachlan was standing over John with his gun aimed. Ready to shoot him for any reason given.

"Ok son, I'll take it from here." The police chief stepped into the room and told John his rights, asked him a few questions but John was unstable. His mind was broken as he said nothing. Together, with stealth I wouldn't think possible, Lachlan and the Chief helped John up to his feet and out to his car without anyone questioning it.

The wedding continued and the highland games started. Everyone was having fun and I was stuck in my head, maybe I'd finally come to my breaking point. I didn't know. When Lachlan finally came back into the room he wrapped his arms around me and I crawled into his lap on the bed.

"It's over baby." I took a deep breath and with my exhale I let go of the fear I had been holding onto. I felt exhausted from all the emotions and adrenaline. I rested my head against Lach's strong chest and listened to his heart beat evenly. He was stable, he was here, and he was my home. I repeated that mantra over and over in my head until I finally felt ok.

"Want to go back out the wedding?" He asked me and I nodded. A distraction. I needed that badly. Together we walked back down to the festivities and I downed the madness of my life in a nice glass of whiskey. Refusing to think of anything heavy for the rest of the day. The blood on the floor in our room could wait. Talking about it could wait. I was alive and right now I wanted to live.

Chapter Twenty-Eight
Lachlan

It had been a two weeks since the wedding. Wolfe and Nera were back on his tour and Lily and I had found a sort of routine in our lives. I got a call for one quick job that was truly one weekend and I was now sitting in the darkness of the stage, waiting to kiss my girl. We'd found peace in the darkness. Her stalker John was getting the help he needed and confessed that he'd gone to extreme lengths to have Lily, which soothed my soul that the purchaser had been caught. Although I still wanted to kill him, I couldn't fault him for losing his mind after losing his wife. I'd be devastated if anything happened to Lily.

There was a crowd of ten students sitting in the front rows as Lily and a man in work out shorts walked on the stage.

"Dance is all about emotion. Provoking it, feeling it, living it. You have until the end of the week to choreograph an emotion piece. I want to feel your every movement." Lily projected her voice towards the teens. She had gotten a position at the local college. Just two classes a week for now but she was taking it very serious.

"Now, Gunner and I are going to demonstrate what I am looking to see from you." She eyed them all before moving towards her position on the stage. The boy Gunner just stood there. He looked to be a student himself, I was curious to see what they would dance to.

A violin along with a piano filled the air, a country voice started singing about a young girl who was anxious to see the doctor. Lily, who was wearing yoga pants and a tight pink camisole started to dance like the young girl in the song. Swaying and twirling around. Her eyes closed as she moved effortlessly hopping from one pointed foot to the other. When the chorus picked up she threw more of herself into her steps. With every flick of her arms, and twist of her torso you felt the emotion of the girl who was diagnosed with cancer and all she wanted was to dance with her first love. When the melody changed speed and the final verses hit, Gunner joins the dance. Lily looked at him like he was her first love, giving up everything to dance with her. He lifted her while she pointed out her leg, spinning her around. Lightly, he placed her down and they twirled around the stage.

I saw a few of the girls sitting in the row wipe away some tears. Lily was damn good evoking emotions through dance. She always had been. When the melody comes to an end Gunner dips her back as she comes into his arms. Holding him tight.

I knew it was all for show, but I still didn't like her in another man's arms.

An applause erupted from the students as Gunner and Lily separated and took a bow.

"Ok, you've got a week to nail down a song and choreography. Get to work!" She says breathlessly to them. She leaned in and thanks Gunner before he jumps off the stage and walks over to join the rest of the kids. Not wanting to wait any longer I stood from the darkness and walked down towards my girl.

She squinted her eyes at my figure through the lights, and once she saw me her face lit up.

She looked at the kids then back at me and made a gesture for me to meet her behind the curtain. My dick stirred thinking about the last time we were on that stage. This time there actually were people in the auditorium so I would have to control myself. I took one step out of the four and was up in seconds. As soon as I pushed back the curtain, Lily's body was on mine. I wasn't prepared for her to jump and cling to me but I reacted quickly.

"You're back." She whispered and held onto me like the floor was going to swallow her up if I set her down.

"I'm home." She looked up at me and those beautiful amethyst eyes were filled with love. Something I'd never thought I would see in my lifetime. She was there fighting back the darkness that tried to surround our souls with her blinding lights of love.

My hands gripped her ass and my lips were on the hunt for hers. She didn't make me chase after them long. I groaned with her lips met mine. She gave her all into the kiss, telling me how much she missed me every day I was gone. Fuck did I miss her.

"What time are you done today?" Wishing she said right now so we could go back to the apartment. We hadn't gotten a place together yet because she was being picky. I couldn't have given a shit but she was looking for something specific. What that was, I had no fucking clue. I just need a place to eat, sleep, shit, and fuck my girl on all of its surfaces. Not a long list of criteria.

"Three. Meet you at the apartment?" She pulled back to see my face when I answered.

"Yeah, my other fiancé wanted me to stop by before you got off work." My silent laughter bubbled over when she smacked me on the arm for teasing her. Things were lighter between us and it was just like old times. Only this time, we would kiss and make up.

"Asshole." She pursed her lips. I set her down and touched her lips with my finger. Trying to ease the tension there by caressing them softly.

"There's no other place I'd rather be than waiting for you to come to me." She bit back a smile and I knew she'd forgiven my tease. She listened to the kids start to get loud, and took a step back from me. Our time right now was over, but later. Nothing was keeping me from showing her just how much I missed her.

"I have to get back to my class, but I'll see you soon." She blew me a kiss and walked back out to her little crew.

I made a stop on the way to the apartment to pick up the engagement ring I'd ordered for her as soon as we left Durness. It was a simple white gold band with one round diamond. The rock was pretty large, 3 carats to be exact. My Starlight deserved something as bright as she was.

The apartment was clean and there was a roast in the crock pot in the kitchen. The feeling of coming home to food cooking and a happy home was still unbelievable. Something that I'm not sure how to get used to. The adrenaline still lingered in my veins from the mission over the weekend. I was jazzed, and playing homemaker was something strange to think about.

I threw my bag on the bed and sat down. Looking at the clock I had a couple hours before Lily would walk through that door, deciding to catch up on some sleep now, so I would have plenty of energy for Lily later. I rolled over and passed out. I would wake before she got home, and if not then she would wake me. Maybe even creatively.

I woke up to the smell of burning roast. Odd. I looked at the clock and saw it was seven pm. Holy shit! Lily didn't wake me up, and I sure as hell didn't. I hopped out of bed and went to see why the house smelled horrible.

"Lily, sorry I slept so late." My fingers ran through my hair, which I'm sure looked like hell.

No answer.

"Lily. Baby?" I looked around and didn't see her. I walked over to the kitchen and looked in the crock pot. It was over cooked. She hasn't been home yet. Immediate anger flooded my system. Did she change her mind? Where the fuck was she? Storming into the bedroom I grabbed my phone and saw nothing. No text, no call. Absolutely nothing. Something wasn't right. Lily wouldn't just leave me without saying something first. Grabbing my keys, I ran out of the apartment and hopped in my car.

Driving faster than I should have, I slammed into the parking lot and tried to find her car. It was gone. She wasn't here. She probably would be pissed at me if she knew but I was thankful as fuck right now that I'd installed a tracker on her car. I pulled up the location on my phone. Her car was in Inverness. What the hell! I called her phone and it went straight to voice mail. Feeling utterly fucked in the head, I got out of the car and tried to calm down. I needed to treat this like any other mission I did. I need my head straight and not to be emotionally charged. Shit went wrong when you went in guns a blazing. I needed to figure out what happened, who happened, and why. The sooner I figured that out the sooner I would get my Lily back.

    The college was closed so there was no one to ask if they had saw her leave with anyone. I went back to the apartment and opened the chest I'd put in the spare bedroom's closet. She didn't know what was in it, and hadn't asked. It was everything that I would need to get her back. I pulled out my computer and fired it up. I hacked into the camera's in the traffic lights on the way from here to Inverness. After running a search on her license plate numbers, it had been caught twice. The passengers on the inside were clouded by darkness so that was useless.

    I ran her credit card numbers through the system, none had been used. Hell. Next, even though I was hoping was a long shot I broke into the airport's system and ran a facial scan with a picture we had gotten at the fairy pools. As the computer did its job, I pulled out my bullet proof vest, and other tactical gear, two hand guns with silencers, two magazine leg holsters, two ankle knife sheaths and a bag full of everything I could need. Gas mask, grenades, cash, energy suckers, and a few other things that would come in handy.

A ding on the screen brought my attention back to the computer's results.

Chapter Twenty- Nine
Lachlan

What I saw burned my very soul. It enraged me and filled my lungs with a curse that couldn't be held inside.

Lily, being dragged by the fucking doctor through the airport. I should have known. John wasn't the purchaser. It was the doctor. But why? Was he bringing her back to his brother? I remembered the way he looked at her and disregarded me. Did he want her? My fists clenched and released in a strenuous pattern for a few minutes. I couldn't lose my shit. Lily needed me. Her face held no panic, but a look of faith. She knew I'd come. I would. I was so fucking going to get her back and shoot him right between the eyes. I might even toy with him a little for putting her through so much shit.

And if he touched her in any way, I would slice his dick off with a butter knife.

I checked into which flight they had taken, Glasgow. Take off was in thirty minutes. I wouldn't need be able to make it the three hours to the airport before they left. I needed something faster. Beat them to Glasgow or be close behind. I ran a search through the database of registered recreational aircrafts in the area. I knew one of these fuckers in this town had something. We had some rich people in the area.

Bingo!

Roger Londel, 65 years old, retired air force vet. Widowed. Two kids in the states and three grandkids.

I closed my computer and shoved it in my bag. One by one I put on my tactical gear. Loading myself up to be the proficient killer I was. I was the best mercenary there was right now. It was the reason I was hired by all sorts of powerful men. I got shit done, and I would succeed in my mission now. After I slid my last knife into its sheath on my ankle, I was done. Tightening my bag around my back, closed up the apartment, and looked around the parking lot. I needed something fast. The sedan I had gotten wasn't fast enough. I walked around and my eyes lit up with excitement. Whipping out my phone, I found the owner of the Ducati bike that was calling to me. I would pay him back for what I was about to do. I found the switch in my bag with the key and quickly switched the ignition to the bike. The key fit perfectly and the bike purred to life. Ready to play.

My leg swung over and fit the black sports bike perfectly. I took off and sped down the road towards Mr. Londel's house. The bike embodied the adrenaline running through me, itching my skin. The darkness shrouded me as I winded through the night and came to my target. I cut the bike off and walked up to the wooden house nestled in the woods. A man who looked fit but tired came out of the door with a shotgun in his hands.

I raised my hands letting him know that I was no harm to him.

"My name is Lachlan Sloan. I need your help, sir." I kept walking as he stood on his porch, pointing his gun right at me.

"What kind of help would you need from a man like me?" His voice was rough and held a bit of a country accent. One I was familiar with since spending time in North Carolina.

"I need to borrow your helicopter, sir. To save my woman." His gun lowered slightly. I kept going.

"She was taken from me and I need to get to her, fast." I stopped at the stairs to his porch. He was five feet away from me. Could shoot me dead right now. But based on what I'd read on him, he would help. Lily's life depended on me being right.

"You can handle her?" I showed no reaction but I was bursting with hope on the inside.

"Very, sir. I can pay you for her. Hourly." I went to reach into my bag with my other hand out so he could see it.

"No need for that. You break her, then your ass owes me a new copter. You ain't got time to tell me about your girl. I'm trusting you, son. If you are lying to me, I'll hunt your ass down." I could tell he truly did believe me. From one man who's killed to another. There were no lies.

"You get her, bring her over. I want to hear this story. Old man ain't got nothing but the copter and trees to occupy my time." He gave me a brief smile before inviting me into the house. He grabbed the keys from a little bowl and tossed them to me. His home was tidy, and something I would expect. There was a bookshelf that had a few pictures of the family he had in the states but not many of him with them. He was a loner.

"Got her back in '82, treat her good, and raise hell." I was a little stunned this was going as smoothly as it was. I expected to pay him for the copter and more, which I could afford. But he didn't want it.

"Thank you, sir. I will bring Lily by." We walked out the back door and over towards a barn and a small opening in a field. I helped him with the help of a tractor roll his 1979 Sikorsky Black Hark military helicopter out of hiding. This retired bastard had one hell of a collector's item.

"Honored, sir." It was the truth. I was honored by him, honored that he would be so open to letting me take his prized possession.

"Without love, there is no life. Get your girl." He walked back out of reach and I climbed into the beast. She started effortlessly, and I prepped her right. After I placed the helmet and head phones, I looked and saw everything, my bag included was ready to go. Roger was standing there, ready to see the takeoff of his beauty. I would owe that man any favor he wanted, and I meant anything.

The bird rose to the sky like she was brand new, and not from the 70's. Probably went through hell and back. But still rose from the ashes.

Once I made it to altitude, I turned her in the direction of Glasgow. Doctor Jarred better have some back up, because I was gunning it for his ass. No amount of guns, nor demons from hell could keep me away from accomplishing this mission. I sent out a silent plea to Lily.

    Hold on, Starlight. I'm coming to get you.

Chapter Thirty
Lily

    I was on a plane with a crazy man. Not really something I ever expected to happen to me in my life but yet it was happening. Jarred, my ex's brother was a psychopath. While I was getting ready to leave work at the school, he stopped by to talk to me and then drugged me. He stuck a syringe right in my neck. Then I woke up in my car, that he was driving on the way to an airport three hours away from Portree. I felt like shit because of the drugs and didn't really feel like I could fight him off and truly, I didn't want to die in a car crash because I was too hasty.

    By the time we got to the airport I was feeling better and could talk but he shut me up really quick.

    "If you make a scene in this airport or try to escape I will one, drug you again, two, have my men, that are on standby, take down your boyfriend's family with one call. Even his little nieces." He looked at me and got out of the car. I was afraid that what he said was true, so I kept my mouth shut and went with him as he dragged me towards the terminal. After grabbing me a coffee and a little snack, we sat and waited for our plane to arrive.

I looked at him sitting next to me on the plane, no one was around us right now and we had some time to kill. I wanted to know why he was doing this. He had always given me the creeps but not in a I'm going to kidnap you kind of way.

"I need some answers." I felt confident enough to talk to him now. He looked at me and smiled inn a loving type of way.

"Of course, I know this is very stressful for you. What would you like to know?" Could he really be this calm about all of this? I wanted to yell at him. Scratch his eyes out, something, anything.

"For starters, why are you doing this?" I'd think it was simple. He pondered over his answer for a minute. I should have known what he was going to say but I wasn't expecting what came out of his mouth.

"I want you, Lily. Always have. I tried to be the nice brother and let Lance have you but I couldn't wait any longer. I had those men take you in Milan. Already paid the fee, and I was going to come get you, nurse you back to health and we would live together. Far away from my family where I could spoil you, take care of you. I tried again with those Italians but they were useless. So I decided if I was going to get anything done, I would have to do it myself." He was still smiling at me, like what he said was supposed to make me fall onto his dick.

"You had me kidnapped three times now, so that we could be together?" It was still incomprehensible to me. I was stunned.

"I'm a man who knows what he wants and has the means to do it. I promise you will have the life you've always dreamed of. We will live somewhere beautiful, like Tuscany, or Australia. You wouldn't have to teach, you could go back to dancing and I can help people anywhere. It will be perfect." He stopped talking to reach out and touch the side of my face. I flinched away from him. Sicko.

"I will never care for you." I spat at him. I didn't understand the way these men were trying to force me to be with them. Then it hit me.

"You were treating John weren't you. You made him believe he was the one to take me so he would take the blame and no one would be the wiser." This man was horrible. Poor John.

"If I didn't do something, that Neanderthal you let spread your legs would have figured it out." He mocked being disgusted when he said Neanderthal.

"Lachlan will come for me. He will find me." He should know that. His hand wrapped around my neck and squeezed hard. Bringing me to an inch away from his lips.

"He won't find us. And if he does. I'll take care of it. I've been dying to hear you scream like you did for him on that stage. He's not going to get in the way of that. No one will." He lips crashed against mine and I wanted to vomit. I bit his tongue when he tried to pry open my mouth with it and heard him groan. My whole entire body convulsed hearing that. God he liked that I was fighting him. Instantly, I shut down and pulled my lips in between my teeth.

"Maybe I'll let him watch this time while I part those pretty dancer thighs. I've been longing to since I saw you." His ick factor just raised to five hundred. He was the stranger that had seen Lachlan and I have sex for the first time on that stage. I felt violated and wronged. If it was just some punk kid, I probably wouldn't have cared but

Jarred sounded like he got off on it. Probably touched himself over me screaming out Lachlan's name. I felt disgusting, and angry.

"You could never make me scream for you like I do for Lachlan. You're a crazy piece of shit." I twisted his hand off of my neck and sat back in my seat. I didn't want to talk to him anymore. All it did was make me feel gross and angry. I had to have faith. Lachlan would find me, and he would kill this asshole.

The rest of the flight was uneventful, I was kind of hoping he would have died or something but alas, that didn't happen. When the plane landed and it was time to get off, he grabbed a bag from the overhead compartment and wrapped his other hand around mine. I tried to shake it off but he just gripped my fingers harder. I winced through the pain as he slowly dragged me down the aisle of seats. I hoped that someone could see through our joined hands and called the cops but everyone was so eager to get off the plane or on their phones that they didn't notice.

"Stop pulling me you're hurting me!" I cursed at him trying to rip my arm away from his.

"I'll fix any injuries later. Right now we need to get to our hotel room for the night and then tomorrow we will head to our temporary home until we figure out where we'd like to live." His creepy love smile was becoming a permanent look on his face. I wanted to take a page from Lachlan's mercenary book and carve his smile like the joker's. We half-jogged to the car rental department, and I kept my mouth shut while he drove us into Glasgow. A city I had been to before for a show, but never really got to look around. I wasn't in awe of the scenery now. I was looking out the window hoping I would see Lachlan.

    When we pulled up to a hotel and parked, I started to get nervous. Would Jarred try and touch me more intimately once we made it inside? I could use my self-defense moves on him, but he said he would kill Lachlan's family. I still believed him, but maybe if I got his phone away from him he couldn't make a call to his men and I could run. The plan started to form in my head as he paid for our room and walked us into the elevator. I could feel the dirty vibes coming off of him in waves. I noticed a small bulge in his slacks from the elevator mirror and wanted to laugh.

    Lachlan had a big dick. Long, always hard for me, and pretty much perfect. He was an animal, a caveman. This creepster thought that he would make me scream like Lachlan? Yeah, right.

When he opened the door his arms nudged me inside as he turned and locked the door. I looked around and noticed it was a simple room. One king size bed, dresser, desk, flat screen TV. The norm.

"I think you need a shower. Long day at school and all the travel. Why don't you go ahead and hop in." He really was crazy if he thought I was getting naked around him. Even if in that shower I would be alone, I would never strip down for him. When I turned to look at him, I should have never said never. He was pointing a gun at me. I was tired of having guns pointed at me.

"Go take a shower, Lily." Slowly my feet moved me towards the bathroom door. I thought about slamming it in his face and locking it but he closed the distance and walked into the bathroom before I had the chance. He closed us in the small space, an eerie feeling crept up my spine.
"I'm not taking a shower with you." I stopped to look at him.

"That's fine. We'll work up to that. Turn the water on." I did as he said and turned to look at him with my arms crossed over my chest. Stupid gun.

"Strip." Those words. Hearing those words come from him while my life was threatened broke away a little of the defiance in me, instead I wanted to cry. I didn't want to show this man any of my body. I didn't want to give in, but I felt like I had no choice. I bit back the plea that was stuck in my throat. I would not beg this man, even though I wanted to. I turned my back to him and started taking off my clothing. I knew he could see the side of me from the mirror over the sinks, but I wasn't going to give him the satisfaction of seeing me tremble before him.

"Get in." His voice had turned gruff and breathy. He was turned on. Stepping into the shower, I reached to close the curtain when his hand stopped it from going further.

"Wash yourself. The curtain stays." Everything I tried to hold back, to not give into him, fell. I did as he said and I cried. He watched me with a heated gaze as I used the hotel's shitty bar of soap to wash my body. Tears fell down my cheeks, mixing with the water's spray. With every shaky breath he took, I fell more inside myself. I closed my eyes and imagined I was on stage. Just another performance. In my head, I was in my happy place. Dancing, feeling the emotions driving me to give it my all. Lachlan was there. Any happy place would include him. I thought about what I would want to say to him, what dance I would do.

Adele's *Make You Feel My Love*. That would be it. With every sway of my body and every twirl he would feel my love for him. How far I would go.

My body may have been in that bathroom being objectified by an evil man, but my mind was on a stage. Giving everything I had into showing Lachlan through my movements, I loved him. Dancing, even in my mind gave me strength. I could handle what Jarred would throw at me. I knew that once all was said and done, I still had love. That he could never take away from me. My body would heal, my mind would forget the pain, and our true love would never die.

I came back to the present and turned off the water. Jarred was rubbing his crotch with his left hand as I turned towards him. I took a step out and wrapped myself up with a towel. My chin held high.

I refused to unwrap myself and dry of the rest of my body. My hair was dripping my back and I couldn't find it in me to care.

He opened the door and I walked through it with him behind me. Just as I heard the door behind us open, I was being yanked into Jarred's arms with his gun to my head and his erection pressed against my ass.

"Leave beast, she's mine." Jarred hissed at the figure. I looked over the brown hair, perfect sharp jaw, and green eyes. He'd found me. Jerking me with him, Jarred walked us back and dug through a bag. I felt a sharp needle close to my neck, turning my blood cold. What did he have in his hands?

"You're going to die." Lachlan spoke calmly, but there was maliciousness in his tone. There was no bargaining with him. He was going to make Jarred pay, in many painful ways.

Jarred pressed the needle into my skin. I yelped but remained still as I felt a foreign liquid rush into my system.

"Now you leave or she dies. I've infected her with hemlock." What the fuck was hemlock? I stared into those green eyes, my serenity. They twitched slightly. Oh god, was hemlock bad? It had to of been.

"I see you know what that is. Well, then you know the plant is the most toxic plant to humans. She'll start to have seizures. Her heart rate will slow, and paralysis will take over. Her body will give up from respiratory failure." He spat from behind me. His dying shield.

"You will save her." Lachlan retorted. I hoped he was right; I really didn't want to die like this.

"Of course I will save her, when you leave and never come back. The choice is yours, kill me now and she dies. Leave and never return and I will save her." My heart started to race and I felt twitches in my fingers. Oh god I was dying. My eyes searched Lachlan's. I was scared. I lost control of my limbs and fell to the floor. Shaking. I closed my eyes and went to my happy place. Dancing for the man I loved. Free.

Chapter Thirty-One
Lachlan

It was Roderick's death all over again. As I stared down at the love of my life, writhing on the floor I was taken back to that warehouse where I had to make a choice. Take a life and save my brother, or refuse and he dies. Only now it was take a life, Lily died. Refuse and she lives. A life without me but she lived. I felt crippled. I heard a bang of a gun and felt a tear by my collar bone. I fell to the ground and stared at her beautifully marred face. She was dying. I looked at the doctor. He thought he had bested me. He'd won. I saw the face of the gang leader all those years ago and did what I couldn't then. I raised my gun and shot him. He deserved more. So much more. As the shock in face fell and his body collapsed to the floor, I felt the biggest of my demons die with him.

I felt blood coat my shoulder. Thank god he was a shit shot and didn't hit me in the head. I pulled out my phone and called for help while searching the doctor's bag for a cure. There were many needles with many meds in there. I wouldn't know how to help even if it was in there.

Crawling over to my Lily, I scooped her into my arms. Her body was still now but her eyes were wide. She was still in there, coherent, but her body was lifeless.

I whispered everything I wished I told her when we were kids. I told her about how she made me feel, and about the time I watched her dance before I left. How I was such an asshat for leaving. I apologized for my stubbornness. I apologized for holding back. But mostly I apologized for not marrying her and giving her a life together earlier.

When the medics arrived and hauled her off to the hospital, I felt myself start to lose consciousness. Whether it was the weight of my choice crashing down on me like a boulder, or I was bleeding out. Maybe both. I'd killed a man and probably lost the love of my life. I prayed to the heavens to save her. She was my angel. My love. She deserved to live her life in happiness. Being an angel to others. I was death, and darkness was consuming me. Take my life to spare hers. I repeated those words over and over until the darkness finally claimed me.

    I stared at the grave before me with a heavy heart. Tears formed in my eyes and I had no choice but to let them loose. I had been gutted, my world had changed so much that day and I wasn't sure it was something I would ever get over. I would live my life. I'd come to peace with my demons but I would never forget the pure agony and soul wrenching pain I'd been through.
    "I know what you're thinking. I didn't do anything wrong. I made the right choice." I started talking to the white tombstone.
    "I get it now. I do. Doesn't mean I don't miss you. Or wish that you were here. You were always so filled with light." I looked at the ground and somehow felt disconnected. I know that was where the coffin actually was but I felt nothing to the ground. The white stone was all I had left.

"But don't worry. I'll be ok now. I may have drifted in the darkness for a long time but I've found my light now. My angel to watch over me." I looked back towards the crowd that had formed by the big oak tree that guarded the cemetery.

Her hair was flowing in the wind as she threw her head back in laughter at something Aiden was saying. My starlight. My angel. She lived and breathed the air around us. I would never be dragged into the dark as long as I had her. Her head turned toward mine and our souls connected. She knew this was hard for me, but yet we came. I looked back at the stone and gestured my head towards Lily.

"You always thought she and I would be good together. You were right. Be at peace brother." I stood and walked toward my world. After the medics had woken me from that hospital bed, I wasn't going to take anything for granted. I waited hours before they had told me that Lily was ok and they saved her. I waited for another four days for her to become conscious again to breathe. Even though she still would get a twitch in her left hand every once in a while all the other symptoms hadn't lingered. She was ok. Her smile grew as I approached until I swept her into my arms. Then her smile brightened with the magnitude of the heavens.

"You ok?" She asked. I leaned down and kissed her. Ignoring my family behind us.

"As long as I have you the light in my life, I will always be ok." I felt the bite of the engagement ring that rested on her left hand on my bicep as she squeezed me.

"Then we are in for a happy rest of our lives because I will always be in your life." She answered and I had finally found peace. No matter what may come our way, we had love and each other. We would conquer it; we would live in the light.

Playlist

Adele- Hello
Mya- My love is like wo
Lee Ann Womack- I hope you dance
Boonie Rait- I can't make you love me
Alison Krauss- When you say nothing at all
Hozier- Cherry wine
Sleeping at last- Turning the page
Drowning Pool- Bodies
Florence and the machine- Heavy in your arms
Adele- Make you feel my love

Acknowledgements

Who do I want to thank first....

I'm going to start with you. The one who picked up my story and decided to give it a shot. Whether you've been a fan of my stories before this one or a new one, I am so thankful for you. You are the best readers an author could ask for.

Next..Hm. Christina, gotta step it up your sister is going to take this spot soon. :P Thank you for your help. You've been there since the beginning.

Cassie, you've helped me so much and I appreciate it so much!

MA, April, Marissa. Thank you so much for helping make sure my story was going to be amazing!

Jennifer, you helped turn my book from a hot mess into something readable. That is huge accomplishment in my book.

Husband and child. You are my rock and I love you so much. Stay cute. Both of you.

About the Author

Jessica Florence, Kaleidoscope of romance. Writer of Surviving Valentine. The of The Heart trilogy, Evergreen, Lights of Scotland series, and The Final KO.

When she's not writing her next invigorating story. You can find her running her own business, and spending time with her husband and daughter in southwest Florida.

Jessica loves to interact with her readers, find her on

https://www.facebook.com/JessicaFlorenceAuthor
Www.JessicaFlorenceAuthor.com
JessicaFlorenceAuthor@gmail.com
https://twitter.com/florence_jess

Made in the USA
Columbia, SC
10 April 2018